Place your initials here to remind you that you have read this book!

The Wyoming Kid

**Center Point
Large Print**

**This Large Print Book carries the
Seal of Approval of N.A.V.H.**

The Wyoming Kid

DEBBIE MACOMBER

CENTER POINT PUBLISHING
THORNDIKE, MAINE

This Center Point Large Print edition
is published in the year 2006 by arrangement with
Harlequin Enterprises Ltd.

The text of this Large Print edition is unabridged. In other
aspects, this book may vary from the original edition.
Printed in the United States of America.
Set in 16-point Times New Roman type.

ISBN 1-58547-797-4

Library of Congress Cataloging-in-Publication Data

Macomber, Debbie.
   The Wyoming kid / Debbie Macomber.--Center Point large print ed.
      p. cm.
   ISBN 1-58547-797-4 (lib. bdg. : alk. paper)
   1. Large type books. I. Title.

PS3563.A2364W96 2006
813'.54--dc22

2006012425

To the Gutsy Girls in the
PAN Group of RWA's Peninsula Chapter

The Wyoming Kid

Chapter One

His truck shuddering as he hit a rut, Lonny Ellison pulled into the ranch yard and slammed on the brakes. He jumped out of the cab, muttering furiously. In pure frustration, he kicked the side of his Ford Ranger with one scuffed boot. His sister, who was hanging clothes on the line, straightened and watched him approach. No word of greeting, not even a wave, just a little smile. As calm as could be, Letty studied him, which only irritated him more. He blamed her for this. She was the one who had her heart set on Lonny's dating that . . . that woman. She was also the one who'd been busy trying to do some matchmaking—not that she'd had any success.

It wasn't like Lonny to let a woman rattle him, but Joy Fuller certainly had. This wasn't the first time, either.

He had plenty of cause to dislike her. Two years ago, when she'd moved to Red Springs to take a teaching job, he'd gone out of his way to make her feel welcome in the community. And how had she responded to his overtures of friendship? She'd thumbed her nose at him! He figured he was well rid of her. They'd argued—he couldn't even remember why—and he hadn't spoken to her since. Until today. Friend of Letty's or not, he wasn't about to let Joy Fuller escape the consequences of what she'd done.

What bothered him most was the complete disre-

9

spect Joy had shown him and his vehicle. Why, his truck was in prime condition, his pride and— No, under the circumstances, he couldn't call it his pride and *joy*. But he treasured that Ford almost as much as he did his horse.

"What's gotten into you?" Letty asked, completely unruffled by his actions.

"Of all the crazy women in the world, why did it have to be *her?*"

"And who would that be?" his sister asked mildly.

"Your . . . your teacher friend. She—" Lonny struggled to find the words. "I'm telling you right now, I'm not letting her get away with this."

Letty's expressive eyes widened and she gave a deep sigh. "For heaven's sake, Lonny, settle down and tell me what happened."

"Look!" he shouted, motioning toward the front of his ten-year-old pickup so his sister could see for herself.

Letty scanned the bumper, but apparently didn't find anything amiss. "What?"

"Here." He pointed, directing her attention to the most recent dent.

"Where?" Letty asked, bending over to examine it more carefully, squinting hard.

"There." If she assumed that being obtuse was amusing him, she was wrong. He stabbed his finger at it again, and then for emphasis ran his hand over it. All right, he'd admit that the truck had its share of nicks and dents. No working rancher drove a vehicle for as many years as he had without collecting a few battle scars. The pickup could use a new front fender, and a paint job wouldn't be a bad idea, but in no way did that minimize what Joy had done.

"This truck is on its last legs, Lonny, or tires, as the case might be."

"You're joking, aren't you? There's another ten years left in the engine." He should've known better than to discuss this with his sister. Women always stuck together.

"You don't mean that tiny dent, do you?" she asked, poking it with her finger.

"Tiny dent!" he repeated, shocked that she didn't see this for what it was. "That *tiny* dent nearly cost me a whole year off my life!"

"Settle down," Letty said again, "and just tell me what happened." She shook her head. "I don't understand why you're so upset."

To say he was *upset* was an understatement. He was fit to be tied, and it was Joy Fuller's fault. Lonny liked to think of himself as an easygoing guy. Very rarely did a woman, any woman, rile him the way Joy had. Not only that, she seemed to enjoy it.

"Joy Fuller ran a stop sign," he explained. "She *claimed* she didn't see it. What kind of idiot misses a stop sign?" Lonny demanded.

"Joy crashed into you?"

"Almost. By the grace of God, I was able to avoid a collision, but in the process I hit the pole."

"What pole?"

He wondered if his sister was doing it on purpose. "The one holding up the stop sign, of course."

Letty just shrugged, which was not the response he was looking for.

Lonny jerked the Stetson off his head, and thrust his fingers through his hair hard enough to pull out several strands. Wincing, he went on with his story. "Then, ever so sweetly, Joy climbs out of her car, tells me she's *sorry* and asks if there's any damage."

"Gee, I hope you slugged her for that," Letty murmured, rolling her eyes.

Lonny decided to ignore the sarcasm. "Right away, I could see the dent, so I pointed it out to her. But that's not the worst of it," he said, not even trying to keep the indignation out of his voice. "She took one look at my truck and said there were so many dents she couldn't possibly know which one our 'minor incident' had caused." His voice rose as his agitation grew. "That's what she called it—a minor incident."

"What did you say next?" Letty asked.

Kicking the dirt with the toe of his boot, Lonny avoided her gaze. "We exchanged a few words," he admitted reluctantly. That was Joy's fault, too. She seemed to expect him to tell her that all was forgiven. Well, he wasn't forgiving her anything, least of all the damage she'd caused.

When he hadn't fallen under her spell as she'd obviously expected, their argument had quickly heated up. Within moments her true nature was revealed. "She said my truck was a pile of junk." Even now the state-

12

ment outraged him. Lonny walked around his Ford, muttering, "That's no way for a lady to talk. Not only did Joy insult my vehicle, she insulted me."

This schoolteacher, this city slicker, had no appreciation of country life. That was what you got when the town hired someone like Joy Fuller. You could take the woman out of the city but there was plenty of city left in her.

"Whatever happened, I'm sure Joy's insurance will take care of it," Letty said in that soothing way of hers.

Lonny scowled. Joy had a lot to atone for as far as he was concerned. He slapped his hat back on his head. "You know what else she did? She tried to buy me off!" Even now, the suggestion offended him. "Right there in the middle of the street, in broad daylight. I ask you, do I look like the kind of guy who can be bribed?"

At Letty's raised eyebrows, Lonny continued. "She offered me fifty bucks."

His sister's mouth quivered, and if he didn't know better, Lonny would've thought she was laughing. "I take it you refused," she murmured.

"You bet I refused," he told her. "There's two or three hundred dollars' damage here. Maybe more."

Letty bent over to examine the bumper a second time. "I hate to say this, but it looks more like a fifty-dollar dent to me."

"No way!" Lonny protested, nearly shocked into silence. He could hardly believe that his own flesh and blood didn't recognize the seriousness of this affront to him and his vehicle.

"It seems to me you're protesting far too loud and long over a silly dent. Joy's managed to get your attention—again. Hasn't she?"

Lonny decided to ignore that comment, which he considered unworthy of his sister. All right, he had some history with Joy Fuller, most of it unpleasant. But the past was the past and had nothing to do with the here and now. "I wrote down her license plate number." He yanked a small piece of paper from his shirt pocket and gingerly unfolded it. "She'll be lucky if I don't report her to the police."

"You most certainly will not!" Letty snatched the paper out of his hand. "Joy is one of my best friends and I won't let you treat her so rudely."

"This isn't the woman you know." His sister hadn't seen the same side of the schoolteacher that he had. "This one's tall with eyes that spit nails. There's an evil look about her—I suspect she normally travels by broomstick."

His sister didn't appreciate his attempt at humor. "Oh, for heaven's sake, Joy plays the organ at church on Sundays. You know her as well as I do, so don't try to pretend that you don't."

"I *don't* know this woman," he announced flatly.

"You have unfinished business with Joy, and that's the reason you're blowing this *incident* out of all proportion."

Lonny thought it best to ignore that comment, too. He'd finished with Joy a long time ago—and she with him—which suited him just fine. "From the look she gave me, I'd say she's one scary woman. Mean as a rat-tlesnake." He gave an exaggerated shiver. "Probably shrinks heads as a hobby."

Letty had the grace to smile. "Would you stop it? Joy's probably the sweetest person I've ever met."

"Sweet?" Lonny hadn't seen any evidence of a gentle disposition. "Do the people of Red Springs realize the kind of woman they're exposing their children to? Someone should tell the school board."

Hands on her hips, Letty shook her head sadly. "I think you've been standing in the sun too long. Come inside and have some iced tea."

"I'm too mad to drink something nonalcoholic. You go on without me." With that, he stalked off toward the barn. Joy Fuller was his sister's friend. One of her best friends. That meant he had to seriously question Letty's taste—and good sense. Years ago, when he was young and foolish, Lonny had ridden broncos and bulls and been known as The Wyoming Kid. He darn near got himself killed a time or two. But he'd rather sit on one of those beasts again than tangle with the likes of Joy Fuller.

Chapter Two

Joy Fuller glanced out the window of her combination third-and-fourth-grade classroom and did a quick double take. It couldn't be! But it was—Lonny Ellison. She should've known he wouldn't just let things be.

The real problem was that they'd started off on the wrong foot two years ago. She'd been new to the community, still learning about life in Red Springs, Wyoming, when she'd met Lonny through a mutual acquaintance.

At first they'd gotten along well. He'd been a rodeo cowboy and had an ego even bigger than that ridiculously big belt buckle he'd shown her. Apparently, she hadn't paid him the homage he felt was his due. After a month or two of laughing, with decreasing sincerity, at his comments about city slickers, the joke had worn thin. She'd made it clear that she wasn't willing to be another of his buckle bunnies and soon after, they'd agreed not to see each other anymore. Not that their relationship was serious, of course; they'd gone out for dinner and dancing a few times—that was about it. So she hadn't thought their disagreement was a big deal, but apparently it had been to Lonny. It seemed no woman had ever spoken her mind to the great and mighty Wyoming Kid before.

Lonny had said he appreciated her honesty, and that was the last she'd heard from him. To be honest, Joy had been surprised by his reaction. However, if that was how he felt, then it was fine with her. He hadn't asked her out again and she hadn't contacted him, either. She saw him around town now and then, but aside from a polite nod or a cool "hello," they'd ignored each other. It was a rather disappointing end to what had begun as a promising relationship. But that was nearly two years ago and she was long past feeling any regrets.

Then she'd had to miss that stop sign and naturally he had to be the one who slammed into the post. The shock of their minor accident—no, incident—still upset her. Worse, Joy hadn't recovered yet from their verbal exchange. Lonny was completely and totally unreasonable, and he'd made some extremely unpleasant accusations. All right, in an effort to be fair, she'd admit that Lonny Ellison was easy to look at—tall and rangy with wide, muscular shoulders. He had strikingly rich, dark eyes and a solid jaw, and he reminded her a little of a young Clint Eastwood. However, appearances weren't everything.

Letty, who was a romantic, had wanted to match Joy with her brother. Letty had only moved to the area this past year and at first she hadn't realized that they'd already dated for a brief time. Joy had done her best to explain why a relationship with Lonny just wouldn't work. He was too stubborn and she was . . . well, a woman had her pride. They simply weren't compatible. And if she hadn't known that before, their near-collision had proven it.

She peeked surreptitiously out the window again. Lonny was leaning against his rattletrap truck, ankles crossed to highlight his dusty boots. Chase Brown, Letty's husband, and Lonny owned adjoining ranches and shared a large herd of cattle. One would think a working rancher had better things to do than hang around outside a schoolyard. He was there to pester her; she was convinced of it. His lanky arms were crossed and his head bowed, with his Stetson riding low on his forehead, as if he didn't have a care in the world. His posture resembled that neon sign of a cowpoke in downtown Vegas, she thought.

She knew exactly why Lonny had come to the school. He was planning to cause her trouble. Joy rued the day she'd ever met the man. He was rude, unreasonable, juvenile, plus a dozen other adjectives she didn't even want to *think* about in front of a classroom full of young children.

Children.

Sucking in a deep breath, Joy returned her attention to her class, only to discover that all the kids were watching her expectantly. Seeing Lonny standing outside her window had thrown her so badly that she'd forgotten she was in the middle of a spelling test. Her students were waiting for the next word.

"Arrogant," she muttered.

A dozen hands shot into the air.

"Eric," Joy said, calling on the boy sitting at the front desk in the second row.

"Arrogant isn't one of our spelling words," he said, and several protests followed.

"This is an extra-credit word," she said. Squinting, she glared out the window again.

No sooner had the test papers been handed in than the bell rang, signaling the end of the school day. Her students dashed out the door a lot faster than they'd entered, and within minutes, the entire schoolyard was filled with youngsters. As luck would have it, she had playground duty that afternoon. This meant she was required to step out of the shelter of the school building and into the vicinity of Lonny Ellison.

Because Red Springs was a ranching community, most children lived well outside the town limits. Huge buses lumbered down country roads every morning and afternoon. These buses delivered the children to school and to their homes, some traveling as far as thirty miles.

Despite Lonny's dire predictions, Joy was surprised by how successfully she'd adjusted to life in this small Wyoming community. Born and raised in Seattle, she'd hungered for small-town life, eager to experience the joys of living in a close, family-oriented community. Red Springs was far removed from everything familiar, but she'd discovered that people were the same everywhere. Not exactly a complicated insight, but it was as profound as it was simple. Parents wanted the best for their children in Red Springs, the same way they did back home. Neighbors were friendly if you made the effort to get to know them. Wyoming didn't have the distinctive beauty associated with Puget Sound and the two mountain ranges; instead, it possessed a beauty all its own. Joy had done her research and was fascinated to learn that this was the land where dinosaurs had once roamed and where more than half the world's geysers were located, in Yellowstone National Park. Much of central Wyoming had been an ancient inland sea, and she'd gone on a few fossil-hunting expeditions with friends from school.

It was true that Joy didn't have access to all the

amenities she did in a big city. But she'd found that she could live without the majority of convenient luxuries, such as movie theaters and the occasional concerts. Movies went to DVD so quickly these days, and if the small theater in town didn't show it, Joy could rent it a few months after its release, via the Internet.

As for shopping, virtually everything she needed was available on-line. Ordering on the Internet wasn't the same as spending the day at the mall, but that, too, had its compensations. If Joy couldn't step inside a shopping mall, then she didn't squander her money on impulse buys.

The one thing she did miss, however, was her family and friends. She talked to her parents every week, and regularly e-mailed her brother and her closest friends. At Christmas or during the summer, she visited Seattle to see everyone. Several of her college classmates were married now. Three years after receiving her master's in education, Joy was still single. While she was in no rush, she did long for a husband and family of her own one day. Red Springs was full of eligible men; unfortunately, most of them were at least fifty. The pickings were slim, as Letty was eager to remind her. She'd dated, but none of the men had interested her the way Lonny once had.

Since there was no avoiding it, Joy left the school and watched as the children formed neat rows and boarded the buses. She folded her arms and stood straight and as tall as her five-foot-ten-inch frame would allow. Thankfully she'd chosen her nicest jumper that morning, a denim one with a white turtleneck. She felt she needed any advantage she could get if she had to face Lonny Ellison. The jumper had buckle snaps and crisscrossed her shoulders, helping to disguise her slight build.

"Miss Fuller, Miss Fuller," six-year-old Cricket Brown shouted, racing across the playground to her side. The first-grader's long braids bounced as she skipped over to Joy. Her cherub face was flushed with excitement.

"Hello, Cricket," Joy said, smiling down at the youngster. She'd witnessed a remarkable change in the little girl since Letty's marriage to Chase Brown. Despite her friendship with Letty, Joy wasn't aware of all the details, but she knew there was a lengthy romantic history between her and Chase, one that had taken place ten years earlier. Letty had moved away and when she'd returned, she had a daughter and no husband.

Letty was gentle, kind, thoughtful, the exact opposite of her brother. Out of the corner of her eye, Joy noticed he was striding toward her.

Cricket wasn't in the line-up for the bus, which explained Lonny's presence. He'd apparently come to pick up his niece. Preferring to ignore him altogether, Joy turned her back to avoid looking in Lonny's direction. The students were all aboard the waiting buses. One had already pulled out of the yard and was headed down the street.

"My Uncle Lonny's here." Cricket grinned ecstatically.

"I know." Joy couldn't very well say she hadn't seen him, because she had. The hair on the back of her neck had stood on end the minute he parked outside the school. The radar-like reaction her body continued to have whenever he made an appearance confused and annoyed her.

"Look! He's coming now," Cricket cried, waving furiously at her uncle.

Lonny joined the two of them and held Joy's look for a long moment. Chills ran down her spine. It was too much to hope that Lonny would simply collect Cricket and then be on his way, too much to hope he wouldn't mention the stop sign incident. Oh no, this man wouldn't permit an opportunity like that to pass him by.

"Mr. Ellison," she said, unwilling to blink. She kept her face as expressionless as possible.

"Miss Fuller." He touched the brim of his Stetson with his index finger.

"Yes?" Crossing her arms, she boldly met his gaze, preferring to let him do the talking. She refused to be intimidated by this ill-tempered rancher. She'd made one small mistake and run a stop sign, causing a *minor* near-accident. The stop sign was new and she'd been so accustomed to not stopping that she'd sailed through the intersection.

She'd driven at the legal speed limit, forgetting about the newly installed stop sign. She'd noticed it at the last possible second; it was already too late to stop but she'd immediately slowed down. Unfortunately, Lonny Ellison had entered the same intersection at the same

22

time and they'd experienced a *trivial* mishap. Joy had been more than willing to admit that she was the one at fault, and she would gladly have accepted full responsibility if he hadn't behaved like an escaped lunatic. In fact, Lonny had carried this incident far beyond anything sane or reasonable.

It didn't help that he was a good five inches taller than she was and about as lean and mean as a wolverine. Staring up at him now, she changed her mind about his being the slightest bit attractive. Well, he *could* be if not for his dark, beady eyes. Even when Joy and Lonny had dated she'd rarely seen him smile. And since then, he seemed to wear a perpetual frown, glaring at her as if she were a stink bug he wanted to stomp.

"I got the estimate on the damage to my truck," he announced, handing her a folded sheet.

Damage? What damage? The dent in his fender was barely visible. Joy decided it was better not to ask. "I'll take a look at it," she said, struggling not to reveal how utterly irritating she found him. As far as she could see, his precious truck was on its way to the scrap yard.

"You'll want to pay particular attention to the cost of repairing that section of the fender," he added.

She might as well pay him off and be done with it. Unfolding the yellow sheet, she glanced down. Despite her best efforts to refrain from any emotion, she gasped. "This is a joke, right?"

"No. You'll see I'm not asking you to replace the *whole* bumper."

"They don't replace half a bumper or even a small

23

section. This . . . this two hundred and fifty dollars seems way out of line."

"A new bumper, plus installation, costs over five hundred dollars. Two hundred and fifty is half of that."

Joy swallowed hard. Yes, she'd been at fault, but even dividing the cost of the bumper, that amount was ridiculous. She certainly hadn't done five hundred dollars' worth of damage—or even fifty dollars, in her opinion.

To his credit, Lonny had done an admirable job of preventing any serious repercussions. She'd been badly shaken by the incident, which could easily have been much worse, and so had Lonny. She'd tried to apologize, sincerely tried, but Lonny had leaped out of his pickup in a rage.

Because he'd been such a jerk about it, Joy had responded in anger, too. From that moment on, they'd had trouble even being civil to each other. Joy was convinced his anger wasn't so much about this so-called accident as it was about their former relationship. He was the one who'd broken it off, not her. Well, okay, it'd been a mutual decision.

Now he was insisting that a mere scratch had cost hundreds of dollars. It was hard to tell which dent the collision had even caused. His truck had at least ten others just like it and most of them were much worse. She suspected he was punishing her for not falling under the spell of the Great Rodeo Rider. *That* was the real story here.

Joy marched over to where Lonny had parked his

vehicle. "You can't expect me to pay that kind of money for one tiny dent." She gestured at the scratched and battered truck. "That's highway robbery." She stood her ground—easy to do because she didn't *have* an extra two hundred and fifty dollars. "What about all the other dents? They don't seem to bother you, but this one does. And why is that, I wonder?"

Anger flashed from his eyes. "That *tiny dent* does bother me. What bothers me more is unsafe drivers. In my view, you should have your driver's license revoked."

"I forgot about the stop sign," Joy admitted. "And I've apologized a dozen times. I don't mean to be difficult here, but this just seems wrong to me. You're angry about something else entirely and we both know what that is."

"You're wrong. This has nothing to do with you and me. This is about my truck."

"Who do you think you're kidding?" she burst out. "You're angry because I'm a woman with opinions that didn't happen to agree with yours. You didn't want a relationship, you wanted someone to flatter your ego and I didn't fall into line the way other women have." She'd never met any of those women, but she'd certainly heard about them. . . .

His eyes narrowed. "You're just a city girl. I'm surprised you stuck around this long. If you figure that arguing will convince me to forget what you did to my truck, you're dead wrong." He shook his head as if she'd insulted him.

Joy couldn't believe he was going to pursue this.

"You owe me for the damage to my vehicle," he insisted.

"You . . . you . . ." she sputtered at the unfairness of it all. "I'm not paying you a dime." If he wanted to be unreasonable, then she could be, too.

"Would you rather I had my insurance company contact yours?"

"Not really."

"Then I'd appreciate a check in the amount of two hundred and fifty dollars."

"That's practically blackmail!"

"Blackmail?" Lonny spat out the word as if it left a bad taste in his mouth. "I went to a lot of time and effort to get this estimate. I wanted to be as fair and amicable as possible and *this* is what I get?" He threw his arms up as if completely disgusted. "You're lucky I was willing to share the cost with you, which I didn't have to do."

"You think you're being *fair?*"

"Yes." He nodded. "I only want to be fair," he said in self-righteous tones.

Joy relaxed. "Then fifty dollars should do it."

Lonny's eyes widened. "Fifty dollars won't even begin to cover the damage."

"I don't see you rushing out for estimates on any of the other damage to your truck." She pointed at a couple of deep gouges on the driver's door.

"I was responsible for those," he said. "I'll get around to taking care of them someday."

"Apparently *someday* has arrived and you're trying to rip me off."

They were almost nose-to-nose now and tall as he was, Joy didn't even flinch. This man was a Neanderthal, a knuckle-dragging throwback who didn't know the first thing about civility or common decency.

"Miss Fuller? Uncle Lonny?"

The small voice of a child drifted through the fog of Joy's anger. To her horror, she'd been so upset, she'd forgotten all about Cricket.

"You're yelling," the little girl said, staring up at them. Her expression was one of uncertainty.

Joy immediately crouched down so she was level with the six-year-old. "Your Uncle Lonny and I let our emotions get the better of us," she said and laughed as if it was all a joke.

Frowning, Cricket glanced from Joy to her uncle. "Uncle Lonny says when you aren't teaching school you shrink heads. When I asked Mom about it, she said Uncle Lonny didn't mean that. You don't really shrink heads, do you?"

Lonny cleared his throat. "Ah, perhaps it's time we left, Cricket." He reached for the little girl's hand but Cricket resisted.

"Of course I don't shrink heads," Joy said, standing upright. Her irritation continued to simmer as she met Lonny's gaze. "Your uncle was only teasing."

"No, I wasn't," Lonny muttered under his breath.

Joy sighed. "*That* was mature."

"I don't care what you think of me. All I want from you is two hundred and fifty dollars to pay for the damage you did to my truck."

"My fifty-dollar offer stands any time you're willing to accept it."

His fierce glare told her the offer was unacceptable.

"If you don't cooperate, I'll go to your insurance company," he warned.

If it came to that, then so be it. Surely a claims adjustor would agree with her. "You can threaten me all you want. Fifty dollars is my best offer—take it or leave it."

"I'll leave it." This was said emphatically, conviction behind each syllable.

Joy handed him back the written estimate. "That's perfectly fine by me. You can contact me when you're prepared to be reasonable."

"You think *I'm* the one who's being unreasonable?" he asked, sounding both shocked and hurt.

She rolled her eyes. Lonny should've had a career as a B-movie actor, not a bull-rider or whatever he'd been. Bull *something,* anyway.

"As a matter of fact, I do," she said calmly.

Lonny had the audacity to scowl.

This man was the most outrageous human being she'd ever had the misfortune to meet. Remembering the child's presence, Joy bit her tongue in an effort to restrain herself from arguing further.

"You haven't heard the last of me," he threatened.

"Oh, say it isn't so," Joy murmured ever so sweetly.

If she never saw the likes of Lonny Ellison again, it would be too soon.

Lonny whirled around and opened the door on the passenger side for his niece.

"Be careful not to scratch this priceless antique," Joy called out to the little girl.

After helping Cricket inside, Lonny closed the door. "Very funny," he said. "You won't be nearly as amused once your insurance people hear from mine."

Joy was no longer concerned about that. Her agent would take one look at Lonny Ellison's beaten-up vehicle and might, if the cowpoke was lucky, offer him fifty bucks.

Whatever happened, he wasn't getting a penny more out of her. She'd rather go to jail.

Chapter Three

"You've got a thing for Miss Fuller, don't you?" Cricket asked as she sat beside Lonny in the cab of his truck. "That's what my mommy says."

Lonny made a noncommittal reply. If he announced his true feelings for the teacher, he'd singe his niece's ears. Joy was right about something, though. His anger was connected to their earlier relationship, if he could even call it that. The first few dates had gone well, and he'd felt encouraged. He'd been impressed with her intelligence and adventuresome spirit. For a time, he'd even thought Joy might be the one. But it became apparent soon enough that she couldn't take a joke. That was when her uppity, know-it-all, schoolmarm side had come out. She seemed to think his ego was the problem. Not so! He was a kidder and she had no sense of humor. He'd been glad to end it right then and there.

His sister had tried to play the role of matchmaker after she returned to Red Springs and became friends with Joy. Lonny wasn't interested, since he'd had a private look into the real Joy Fuller, behind all her sweetness and charm.

"Mom says sometimes people who really like each other pretend they don't, 'cause they're afraid of their feelings," Cricket continued, sounding wise beyond her years. He could hear the echo of Letty's opinions in her daughter's words.

Leave it to a female to come up with a completely nonsensical notion like that.

"Do you like Miss Fuller the way Mom said?" Cricket asked again.

Lonny shrugged. That was as much of a comment as he cared to make. He was well aware of his sister's opinions. Letty hoped to marry him off. He was thirty-five now, and the pool of eligible women in Red Springs was quickly evaporating. His romantic sister had set her sights on him and Joy, but as far as he was concerned, hell would freeze over first.

Lonny figured he'd had his share of women on the rodeo circuit and he had no desire for that kind of complication again. Most of those girlfriends had been what

30

you'd call short-term—some of them *very* short-term. They'd treated him like a hero, which was gratifying, but he'd grown tired of their demands, and even their adulation had become tiresome after a while. Since he'd retired six years earlier, he'd lived alone and frankly, that was how he liked it.

Just recently he'd hired Tom, a young man who'd drifted onto his ranch. That seemed to be working out all right. Tom had a room in the barn and kept mostly to himself. Lonny didn't want to pry into his business, but he had checked the boy's identification. To his relief, Tom was of age; still, he seemed young to be completely on his own. Lonny had talked to the local sheriff and learned that Tom wasn't wanted for any crimes. Lonny hoped that, given time, the boy would trust him enough to share what had prompted him to leave his family. For now, he was safer living and working with Lonny than making his own way in the world.

Despite his sister's claims, Lonny was convinced that bringing a woman into his life would cause nothing but trouble. First thing a wife would want to do was update his kitchen and the appliances. That stove had been around as long as he could remember—his mother had cooked on it—and he didn't see any need to buy another. Same with the refrigerator. Then, as soon as a wife had sweet-talked him into redoing the kitchen, sure as hell she'd insist on all new furniture. It wouldn't end there, either. He'd be forking out for paint and wallpaper and who knows what. After a few months he wouldn't even recognize his own house—or his bank account. No, sir, he couldn't afford a wife, not with the financial risk he and Chase were taking by raising their cattle without growth hormones.

A heifer took five years to reach twelve hundred pounds on the open range, eating a natural diet of grass. By contrast, commercial steers, who were routinely fed hormones, reached that weight in eighteen to twenty months. That meant they were feeding and caring for a single head of beef nearly three years longer than the average cattleman. Penned cattle were corn-fed and given a diet that featured protein supplements. Lonny had seen some of those so-called supplements, and they included chicken feathers and rot like that. Furthermore, penned steers were on a regimen of antibiotics to protect them from the various diseases that ran rampant in such close quarters.

Yup, they were taking a risk, he and Chase, raising natural beef, and the truth was that Lonny was on a tight budget. But he could manage, living on his own, even with Tom's wages and the room and board he provided. Lonny was proud of their cattle-ranching venture; not only were they producing a higher quality beef, for which the market was growing, but their methods were far more humane.

Cricket sang softly to herself during the rest of the ride. Lonny pulled into the long dirt drive that led to Chase and Letty's place, leaving a plume of dust in his wake.

When he neared the house, he was mildly surprised to

find Chase's truck parked outside the barn. His sister had phoned him a couple of days earlier and asked him to collect Cricket after school. Letty had an appointment with the heart specialist in Rock Springs, sixty miles west of Red Springs. Chase had insisted on driving her. Of course Lonny had agreed to pick up his niece.

Letty had undergone heart surgery a little less than a year ago. While the procedure had been a success, she required regular physicals. Lonny was happy to help in any way he could. He knew Letty was fine health-wise, and in just about every other way, too. In fact, he'd never seen his sister happier. Still, it didn't do any harm to have that confirmed by a physician.

As soon as he eased the truck to a stop, Cricket bounded out of the cab and raced off to look for her mother. Lonny climbed out more slowly and glanced around. He walked into the barn, where Chase was busy with his afternoon chores.

"Cricket's with you?" Chase asked, looking up from the stall he was mucking out.

Lonny nodded. "Letty asked me to pick her up today."

Straightening, Chase leaned against the pitchfork and slid back the brim of his hat. "Why'd she do that?" he asked, frowning slightly. "The school bus would've dropped her off at your place. No need for you to go all the way into town."

"I had other business there," Lonny said, but he didn't explain that his real reason had to do with Joy Fuller and the money she owed him.

"Hey, Lonny," Letty called. Bright sunlight spilled into the barn as Letty swept open the door. Cricket stayed close to her mother's side. "I wondered if I'd find you here."

"I thought you might want your daughter back," he joked. "How'd the appointment go?"

"Just great." She raised her eyebrows. "Cricket tells me you got into another argument with Joy."

He frowned at his niece. He should've guessed she'd run tattling to her mother. "The woman's being completely unreasonable. Personally, I don't know how you can get along with her."

"Really?" Letty exchanged a knowing look with her husband.

"Just a minute here!" Lonny waved his finger at them. "None of that."

"None of what?" His sister was the picture of innocence.

"You know very well what I mean. You've got this sliver up your fingernail about me being attracted to your friend, and how she'd be the perfect wife."

"You're protesting too much." Letty seemed hard put to keep from rubbing her hands together in satisfaction. His sister was in love and it only made sense, he supposed, for her to see Cupid at work between him and Joy. Only it wasn't happening. He didn't even like the woman.

Not that there was any point in further protest. Arguing with his sister was like asking an angry bronc not to throw you. No matter what Lonny said or did, it wouldn't change Letty's mind. Despite their brief and ill-fated romance, something—he couldn't imagine what—had convinced his softhearted little sister that he was head-over-heels crazy about Joy.

"What did you say to her *this* time?" Letty demanded.

"Me?"

"Yes, you!" She propped her hands on her hips, and judging by her stern look, there was no escaping the wrath of Letty. The fact that Joy had managed to turn his own sister against him was testament to the evil power Joy Fuller possessed.

"If you must know, I took her the estimate for the damage she did to my truck."

"You're kidding!" Letty cried. "You actually got an estimate?"

"Damn straight I did." Okay, so maybe he was carrying this a bit far, but someone needed to teach this woman a lesson, and that someone might as well be him.

"But your truck . . ."

Lonny already knew what she was going to say. It was the same argument Joy had given him. "Yes, there are plenty of other dents on the bumper. All I'm asking is that she make restitution for the one *she* caused. I don't understand why everyone wants to argue about this. She caused the dent. The least she can do is pay to have it fixed."

"Lonny, you've got to be joking."

He wasn't. "What about assuming personal responsibility? You'd think a woman teaching our children would *want* to make restitution." According to Letty, the entire community thought the sun rose and set on Miss Fuller. Not him, though. He'd seen the woman behind those deceptive smiles.

"What did Joy have to say to that?" Chase asked, and his mouth twitched in a smile he couldn't quite hide.

Lonny resisted the urge to ask his brother-in-law what he found so darned amusing. "She made me an insulting offer of fifty dollars. The woman's nuts if she thinks I'll accept that."

Letty uttered a rather unfeminine-sounding snort. "I can't say I blame her."

His own sister had sided with Joy and against him. Lonny was sad to see it. "What about my truck? What about me? That woman's carelessness nearly gave me a heart attack!"

"She said she apologized."

Obviously Joy had gone directly to his sister telling tales. Granted, after the accident, Joy had been all sweet and apologetic. However, it didn't take long for her dark side to show, just like it had two years ago.

Since everyone was taking sides with Joy, Lonny considered dropping the entire matter. For a moment, anyway . . . When he presented Joy with the bill, he'd hoped she'd take all the blame and tell him how sorry she was . . . and sound as if she meant it. At that point, he would've felt good about absolving her and being magnanimous. He'd figured they could talk like adults, maybe meet for a friendly drink—see what happened from there.

That, however, wasn't how things had gone. Joy had exploded. His impetuous little fantasy shriveled up even more quickly than it had appeared, to be replaced by an anger that matched hers.

"What are you planning to do now?" Letty asked, checking her watch.

Lonny looked to his brother-in-law and best friend for help, but Chase was staying out of this one. There was a time Chase would've leaped to Lonny's defense. Not now; marriage had changed him. "I don't know yet. I was thinking I should file a claim with her insurance company." He didn't really plan to do that, but the threat sounded real and he'd let Letty believe he just might.

"You wouldn't dare," his sister snapped.

He shrugged, afraid now that he was digging himself into a hole. But pride demanded he not back down.

"One look at your truck and I'm afraid the adjustor would laugh," Chase told him.

That hole was getting deeper by the minute.

Shaking her head, Letty sighed. "I'd better call Joy and see if she's okay."

Lonny stared at her. "Why wouldn't she be okay?"

Letty patted his shoulder. "Sometimes you don't know how intimidating you can be, big brother. Chase and I know you're a pussycat, but Joy doesn't."

As Lonny stood there scratching his head, wondering how everything had gotten so confused, Letty walked out of the barn.

Utterly baffled, Lonny muttered, "Did I hear her right? Is she actually going to phone Joy? Isn't that like consorting with the enemy? What about family loyalty, one for all and all for one, that kind of stuff?"

Chase seemed about to answer when Letty turned back. "Do you want to stay for dinner?" she asked.

Invitations on days other than Sunday were rare, and Lonny had no intention of turning one down. He might be upset with his sister but he wasn't stupid. Letty was a mighty fine cook. "Sure."

A half hour or so later, Lonny accompanied his brother-in-law to the house. After washing up, Chase brought out two cans of cold beer. Then, just as they had on so many other evenings, the two of them sat on the porch, enjoying the cool breeze.

"The doc said Letty's going to be all right?" Lonny asked his friend.

Chase took a deep swallow of beer. "According to him, Letty's as fit as a fiddle."

That was what Lonny had guessed. His sister had come home after ten years without telling him why— that her heart was in bad shape. She'd needed an expensive surgery, one she couldn't afford, and she'd trusted Lonny to raise Cricket for her when she died. Cricket's father had abandoned Letty before the little girl was even born. Letty hadn't told Lonny any more than that, and he'd never asked. Thankfully she'd had the surgery and it'd been successful. She was married to Chase now; even for a guy as cynical about marriage as Lonny, it was easy to see how much she and

Chase loved each other. Cricket had settled down, too. For the first time in her life, the little girl had a father and a family. Lonny was delighted with the way everything had turned out for his sister and his best friend.

"You like married life, don't you?" he asked. Although he knew the answer, he asked the question anyway. Lonny couldn't think of another man who'd be completely honest with him.

Chase looked into the distance and nodded.

"Why?"

Chase smiled. "Well, marriage definitely has its good points."

"Sex?"

"I'm not about to discount that," his friend assured him, his smile widening. "But there's more to marriage than crawling into bed with a warm body."

"Such as?"

Chase didn't take offense at the question, the way another guy might have. "I hadn't realized how lonely it was around this place since my dad died," Chase said. His expression was sober and thoughtful as he stared out at the ranch that had been in his family for four generations. "Letty and Cricket have given me purpose. I have a reason to get out of bed in the morning—a reason other than chores. That's the best I can explain it."

Lonny leaned back and rested his elbows on the step. He considered what his friend had said and, frankly, he didn't see it. "I like my life the way it is."

Chase nodded. "Before Letty returned, I thought the same thing."

At least *one* person understood his feelings.

"Is it okay if I join you?" Letty asked from behind the screen door before moving on to the porch. She held a tall glass of lemonade.

"Sure, go ahead," Lonny said agreeably.

His sister sat on the step beside Chase, who slid his arm around her shoulder. She pressed her head against him, then glanced at Lonny.

"Did you phone her?" It probably wasn't a good idea to even ask, but he had to admit he was curious.

"I will later," Letty said. "I was afraid if I called her now, she might be too distressed to talk."

"I'm the one who's distressed," he muttered, not that anyone had asked about *his* feelings.

Letty ignored the comment. "You've really got a thing for her, don't you?"

"No, I don't." Dammit, he wished his sister would stop saying that. Even his niece was parroting her words. Lonny didn't want to argue with Letty, but the fact was, he knew his own feelings. "I can guess what you're thinking and I'm here to tell you, you're wrong."

"You seem to talk about her quite a bit," she said archly.

No argument there. "Now, listen, I want you to give me your solemn word that you won't do anything stupid."

"Like what?" Letty asked.

"Like try to get me and Joy together again. I told you before, I'm not interested and I mean it."

"You know, big brother, I might've believed you earlier, but I don't anymore."

Not knowing what to say, Lonny just shook his head. "I want your word, Letty. I'm serious about this."

"Your brother doesn't need your help." Chase kissed the top of her head.

"He's right," Lonny said.

"But—"

"I don't need a woman in my life."

"You're lonely."

"I've got plenty of friends, plus you guys practically next door," he told her. "Besides, Tom's around."

At this reminder of the teenage boy living at the ranch, Letty asked, "How's that going?"

Lonny shrugged. "All right, I guess." He liked the kid, who was skinny as a beanpole and friendly but still reserved. "He's a hard worker."

Letty reached for Chase's hand. "It was good of you to give him a job."

Lonny didn't think of it that way. "I was looking for seasonal help. He showed up at the right time." When Lonny found him in the barn, Tom had offered to work in exchange for breakfast. The kid must've been half-starved, because he gobbled down six eggs, half a pound of bacon and five or six slices of toast, along with several cups of coffee. In between bites, he brushed off Lonny's questions about his history and hometown. When Lonny mentioned that he and Chase were hoping to hire a ranch hand for the season, Tom's eyes had brightened and he'd asked to apply for the job.

"I'm worried about you," his sister lamented, refusing to drop the subject. "You do need someone."

"I do not."

Letty studied him for a long moment, then finally acquiesced. "Okay, big brother, you're on your own."

And that was exactly how Lonny wanted it.

Chapter Four

Tom Meyerson finished the last of his nightly chores and headed for his room in the barn. Stumbling onto this job was the best thing that'd happened to him in years. He'd been bone-weary and desperate when Lonny Ellison found him sleeping in his barn. That day, three months ago now, he'd walked twenty or twenty-five miles, and all he'd had to eat was an apple and half a candy bar. By the time he saw the barn far off in the distance, he'd been thirsty, hungry and so exhausted he could barely put one foot in front of the other. He didn't think he'd make it to the next town by nightfall, so he'd hidden in the barn and fallen instantly asleep.

Life had been hell since his mother died. The doctor had said she had a weak heart, and Tom knew why: his dad had broken it years before. His father was a no-good drunk. There'd been nothing positive in Tom's life except his mother. Fortunately, he was an only child, so at least there wasn't a younger brother or sister to worry about. Shortly after he graduated from high school last spring, nearly a year ago, it became apparent that his father's sole interest in him was as a source of beer money. He'd stolen every penny Tom had tried to save.

The last time his money had mysteriously disappeared, Tom had confronted his father. They'd had a vicious argument and his old man had kicked him out of the house. At first Tom didn't know what to do, but then he'd realized this was probably for the best. He collected what was due him from the hardware store where he worked part-time and, with a little less than fifty dollars in his pocket, started his new life. He'd spent twenty of those dollars on a bus ticket to the town of Red Springs, then walked from there. All Tom wanted was to get away from Thompson, Wyoming, as far and fast as he could. It wasn't like his father would be looking for him.

Life on the road was hard. He'd hitchhiked when he could, but there'd been few vehicles on the routes he'd traveled. Most of the time he'd hoofed it. He must have walked a hundred miles or more, and no matter what happened, he never wanted to go back.

When Lonny Ellison discovered him, Tom was sure the rancher would file trespassing charges. Instead, Lonny had given him a job, a room and three square meals a day, which was more than he'd had since his mother's death.

The phone in the barn rang, and Tom leaped out of his bunk where he'd been reading yesterday's paper and hurried to answer it. Lonny wasn't back from town yet, he noticed, because his truck wasn't parked out front.

He lifted the receiver and offered a tentative, "Hello."

A short silence followed. "Tom?"

Tom's heart began to pound. It was Michelle, a girl he'd met at the feed store soon after he'd started working for Lonny. Like him, she was shy and although they hadn't said more than a few words to each other, he enjoyed seeing her. Whenever he went to the store with Lonny, she made an excuse to come out of the office and hang around outside.

"Hi." Tom couldn't help being excited that she'd phoned.

"You didn't come in this afternoon," Michelle said, sounding disappointed.

Tom had looked forward to seeing her all week, only to be thwarted. "Lonny decided to drive into town by himself." Tom had searched for an excuse to join him, but none had presented itself, so he'd stayed on the ranch. He liked the work, although he'd never lived on a ranch before, and Lonny and Chase were teaching him a lot.

His afternoon had been spent repairing breaks in the fencing along the road. The whole time he was doing that, he was thinking about Michelle and how pretty she was.

"I wondered," Michelle whispered, then hesitated as if there was more she wanted to tell him.

Her father owned Larson's Feed, and she helped out after school. The last time he was in town, he'd casually mentioned that he'd be back on Tuesday and hoped to see her. He wanted to ask her out on a date but didn't have any way of getting into Red Springs without borrowing Lonny's truck and he was reluctant to ask. Lonny had already done plenty for him, and it didn't seem right to take advantage of his generosity.

"Lonny had to pick up his niece after school," Tom added.

"Oh."

Michelle didn't appear to be much of a conversationalist, which could be a problem because he wasn't, either.

"I was hoping, you know . . ." She let the rest fade. Then, all at once, she blurted out, "There's a dance the last day of school. It's a pretty big deal. The whole town throws a festival and the high school has this big dance and I was wondering if you'd go with me."

She said it all so fast, she couldn't possibly have taken a breath. After she finished speaking, it took Tom a few seconds to realize what she'd asked him. He felt an immediate surge of regret.

The silence seemed endless as he struggled with what to tell her. In the end, he told the simple truth. "I can't."

"Why not?"

Tom didn't want to get into that. "I just . . . can't." He hated to disappoint her, but there was nothing more he could say.

"I shouldn't have asked . . . I wouldn't have, but— Oh, never mind. I'm sorry. . . ." With that, she hung up as if she couldn't get off the line fast enough.

Tom felt wretched. He didn't have the clothes necessary for any dance; in fact, he'd never attended a dance in his life, even in high school. Those kinds of social events were for other kids. He was sorry to refuse Michelle, sorrier than she'd ever know, but there wasn't any alternative.

As he returned to his room, Tom lay back on the hard mattress and tucked his hands behind his head, staring up at the ceiling. It would've been nice, that school dance with Michelle. All they'd done so far was talk a few times. The thought of holding her in his arms imbued him with a sense of joy—a joy that was unfamiliar to him.

Tom gave himself a mental shake. He might as well forget about the dance right then and there, because it wasn't going to happen. His joy quickly disappeared.

JUST BACK FROM SCHOOL, Joy was still furious over her confrontation with Lonny Ellison. The man had his nerve. In an effort to forget that unfortunate episode, Joy tried to grade the spelling-test papers, but she soon discovered she couldn't concentrate. The only thing she seemed able to do with all this pent-up anger was pace her living room until she'd practically worn a pattern in the carpet.

When the phone rang, Joy nearly jumped out of her skin. Her heart still hadn't stopped hammering when she picked up the portable telephone on the kitchen counter.

"Joy, it's Letty. Lonny dropped Cricket off and he's beside himself. What happened?"

"Your brother," Joy answered from between gritted teeth, "is the most egotistical, unpleasant, arrogant man I've ever met." Then she proceeded to describe the entire scene, which was burned in her memory.

"You mean to say you didn't *really* come after him with a pitchfork?" Letty asked.

"Is that what he said?" Joy asked. She wouldn't put it past Lonny to fabricate such a ridiculous story.

"No, no, I was just teasing," Letty assured her. "But I will say his version of events is only vaguely similar to yours."

"He's exaggerating, of course."

"I apologize," Letty said, sounding genuinely contrite. "I wish I knew what's gotten into my brother. My guess is that he's attracted to you and isn't sure how to deal with it. What happened with you two, anyway?"

"I don't know, and furthermore, I don't care." That wasn't completely true. She did care and, despite her annoyance with his current attitude, wished the situation between them was different.

Letty hesitated briefly before she continued. "I have no idea how else to explain my brother's behavior. All I can tell you is that this just isn't like Lonny."

"In other words, it's me he dislikes." Her heart sank with this.

"No," Letty said. "Just the opposite. I think this is his nutty way of getting back together with you. Like I said, he's attracted to you. There's no question in my mind about that."

Her ego would like to believe it, but she'd seen the

look in Lonny's eyes and it wasn't admiration or attraction.

"Lonny can be a little stubborn but—"

"A little?" Joy broke in. "A *little?*"

"I apologize on his behalf," Letty said. "I'm just hoping you'll be able to look past his perverse behavior and recognize the reason for it. Be gentle with him, okay? I'm fairly certain my brother is smitten."

"He's what?"

"Smitten," Letty repeated. "It's an old-fashioned word, one my mother would've used. It means—well, you know what it means. The sad part is, Lonny isn't smart enough to figure this out."

"Then I hope he never does, because any spark of interest I might've felt toward him is dead. No one's ever made me so mad!" Joy felt her anger gain momentum and crowd out her other feelings for Lonny.

"You're *sure* you're not interested in my brother?"

"Positive. I don't want to see him again as long as I live. Every time I do, my blood pressure rises until I feel like my head's going to explode. I've never met a more irritating man in my life."

Letty's regretful sigh drifted through the phone line. "I was afraid of that."

They spoke for a few more minutes and then Joy replaced the receiver. She felt better after talking to Letty—only she wasn't sure why. Maybe venting her aggression with someone who understood both her and Lonny had helped. It would be nice, flattering really, if all this craziness was indeed related to Lonny's over-

powering attraction, as Letty seemed to think, but Joy wasn't foolish enough to believe it.

Joy hadn't been on a date in so long that she was actually considering one of those on-line dating services. School would be out in a couple of weeks; this summer, when she had some free time, Joy planned to develop a social life. She didn't have a strategy yet, beyond the vague possibilities offered by the Internet, nor did she have much romantic experience. Her only serious romance had been with Josh Howell in her last year of college. Their relationship was relegated to casual friends status after she'd accepted this teaching job in Wyoming. They kept in touch and occasionally e-mailed each other. Since she'd moved away, he'd been involved in an increasingly serious relationship. She hadn't heard from him in more than two months, and Joy surmised that his current girlfriend was soon to become his wife.

Josh lived in Seattle, where he worked for an investment firm. He went on—in detail—about the woman he was seeing every time he e-mailed her. Lori Something-or-Other was apparently blond, beautiful and a power to be reckoned with in the investment industry. Or maybe it was insurance . . . In any case, Joy sometimes wondered why he kept in touch with her at all when he was so enamored of someone else.

Joy microwaved a frozen entrée for dinner, ate while watching the national news, corrected her spelling test papers and then logged on to the Internet. She immediately noticed Josh's e-mail. How ironic that she'd get

this message when she'd just been thinking about him.

From: Josh Howell
Sent: May 16
To: Joy Fuller
Subject: I'm going to be in your area!
Hi, Joy,
We haven't exchanged e-mails in a while, and I was wondering what you've been up to lately. The company's sending me on a business trip to Salt Lake City, which I'm combining with a few vacation days. When I looked at the map, I noticed that Red Springs isn't too far away. I'd love to stop by and catch up with you. After the conference, I'll rent a car, and I should be in your area the first or second of June. Would that work for you?

Looking forward to hearing from you! I've missed your e-mails.
Love,
Josh
P.S. Did I mention that Lori and I broke up?

With her hand pressed to her mouth to contain her surprise and happiness, Joy read the e-mail twice. Josh wasn't seeing Lori anymore! Interesting that he'd mentioned it in a postscript, as if he'd almost forgotten the fact. This made her wonder. Had she misinterpreted the extent of his feelings for the other woman? Did he still consider Joy more than just a friend? Was he suggesting

50

they might want to pick up the relationship where they'd left off? She was certainly open to the possibility. Josh was a man who knew how to treat a woman. He could teach Lonny Ellison a thing or two.

Another interesting fact—Josh had said he'd be in the area, but Red Springs was a little out of his way. Like about two hundred miles . . . Not that she was complaining. What she suspected, what she wanted to believe, was that he'd go a *lot* out of his way in order to see her.

Joy quickly e-mailed Josh back. In the space of a single evening, her emotions had veered from fury to eager anticipation. Earlier she'd had to resist the urge to burst into tears, and now she was bubbling with delight.

Just before hitting Send, Joy paused. Maybe she should phone Josh instead. It wouldn't hurt. Calling him meant he'd know without a doubt how pleased she was to hear from him.

She hesitated, suddenly worried that she might seem too eager. But she was. In fact, she was thrilled. . . .

Her mind made up, she reached for the phone. If he didn't answer, she could always send the e-mail she'd already composed. Receiver in hand, Joy realized she no longer remembered his number. She'd written it down, but had no idea exactly where. Still, she found it easily enough, at the very back of her personal phone directory. In pencil, which implied that she'd expected to erase it. . . .

Josh answered right away.

"Josh, it's Joy. I just opened your e-mail."

"Joy!" She could hear the smile in his voice.

"I'd love it if you came to Red Springs, but I need to warn you we're in the middle of nowhere. Well, not really . . . There *are* other towns, but they're few and far between." She was chattering, but it felt so good to talk to him. "One of my teaching friends said we may not be at the end of the world, but you can see it from here."

Josh responded with a husky laugh. "How are you?"

"Great, just great." Especially now that she'd heard from him.

"Do those dates work for you?" he asked.

Joy had been so excited, she hadn't even checked the calendar. A glance at the one on her desk showed her that June first fell on a Thursday and the second . . .

"June second is the last day of school," she told him, her hopes deflating.

"That's fine. I'll take you out to dinner and we can celebrate."

"There's a problem. On the evening of the last day, we have a big carnival. The whole town shows up. It's sort of a big deal, and this year they've even managed to get a real carnival company to set up rides. Everyone's looking forward to it."

"So we'll attend the carnival."

That sounded good, except for one thing. "I'm working the cotton candy machine." She'd taken that task the year before, too. While it'd been a lot of fun, she'd worn as much of the sugary pink sweetness as she'd managed to get onto the paper tubes.

"Not to worry, I'll find something to occupy myself

while you're busy. If the school needs another volunteer, sign me up. I'm game for just about anything."

"You'd do that?" This was better than Joy would have dreamed. "Thanks! Oh, Josh, I can't tell you how glad I am to hear from you."

"I feel the same way."

"I'm sorry about you and Lori," she said, carefully broaching the subject.

His hesitation was only slight; still, Joy noticed. "Yeah," he said. "Too bad it didn't work out."

He didn't supply any details and Joy didn't feel it would be right to question him. Later, when they were able to meet and talk face-to-face, he'd probably be more comfortable discussing the circumstances of their parting.

"How's life in cowboy town?" Josh asked, changing the subject. When she'd been offered the teaching position, he'd discouraged her from accepting it. Josh had told her she shouldn't take the first job offered. He was convinced that if she waited, there'd be an opening in the Seattle area. He couldn't understand why Joy had wanted to get away from the big city and live in a small town.

The truth was, she loved her job and Red Springs. This was the second year of a two-year contract and, so far, she'd enjoyed every minute. That didn't mean, however, that she wouldn't be willing to move if the opportunity arose—such as renewing a promising relationship, with the hope of a marriage proposal in the not-so-distant future.

"They seem to grow cowboys by the bushel here," she said with a laugh. "Most of the kids are comfortable in the saddle by the time they're in kindergarten. I like Red Springs, but I'm sure that to outsiders, the town isn't too impressive. There are a couple of nice restaurants, the Mexican Fiesta and Uncle Dave's Café, but that's about it."

He murmured a noncommittal response.

"The town seemed rather bleak when I first arrived." She didn't mention the disappointing relationship with Lonny Ellison—then or now. "That didn't last long, though. It's the people here who are so wonderful." With one exception, she mused. "We've got a motel— I'll make a reservation—a couple of bars, a great church, a theater and—"

"Do you still play the church organ?"

"I do." She was surprised he'd remembered that.

"Anything else I should know about Red Springs?"

"Not really. I'll be happy to give you the grand tour." The offer was sincere. She'd love showing off the town and introducing him to the friends she'd made. "Maybe we can visit a real working ranch—my friend Letty's, for example. We could even do that on horseback."

"Don't tell me you're riding horses yourself?"

"I have," she answered, smiling. "But I don't make a habit of it." Getting onto the back of a horse had been daunting the first time, but Joy discovered she rather enjoyed it. Well . . . she didn't hate it. Her muscles had been sore afterward and she hadn't felt the urge to try it again for quite a while. She'd gone out riding with friends three times in the last nine months, and that was enough for her.

"I don't suppose any of those cowpokes have caught your interest," Josh said casually.

Lonny Ellison instantly flashed across her mind. She squeezed her eyes shut, unnerved by the vividness of his image.

"So there *is* someone else," Josh said when she didn't immediately respond.

"No." She nearly swallowed her tongue in her eagerness to deny it. "Not at all."

"Good," Josh said. It seemed he'd decided to accept her denial at face value, much to Joy's relief. She *wasn't* interested in Lonny Ellison, so she hadn't lied. Annoyed by him, yes. Interested? No, no, no! "I'll be in touch again soon," he was saying.

"I'll see you in a couple of weeks." Joy could hardly wait.

Chapter Five

Saturday morning, Lonny woke in a surprisingly good mood. For some reason, he'd dreamed about Joy Fuller, although it'd been several days since he'd run into her. He was reluctant to admit it, but he hadn't been as annoyed by their confrontation as he'd let her believe.

He frowned at the thought. Could it be that Letty was right and he was still attracted to Joy? Nah. Still, the possibility stayed in his mind. One thing was certain;

he'd felt invigorated by their verbal exchanges and he seemed to think of her all too frequently.

He poured his first cup of coffee and stepped outside, taking a moment to appreciate the early-morning sunlight that greeted him. A rooster's crowing accentuated the feeling of peace and contentment. This was his world, the only place he wanted to be.

The one thing that troubled him on what should've been a perfect spring day was the way Joy Fuller lingered in his mind. He couldn't stop remembering how pretty she was and how animated she got when she was all riled up. He shouldn't be thinking about her at all, though. He had chores to do, places to be and, most importantly, cattle to worm. But with Tom's help, they'd make fast work of it. Chase had already done some of the herd the day before.

It was unfortunate that he and Joy had gotten off on the wrong foot, he thought as he scattered grain for the chickens. He discovered a dozen eggs waiting for him, and that made him smile.

But he was irritated when he found himself continuing to smile—smiling for no real reason. Well, there *was* a reason and her name was Joy Fuller and that was even worse. He was a little unnerved by his own amusement at her reaction to his outrageous comments. He'd never had any intention of contacting his insurance company or hers. In the light of day, he realized how irrational he'd sounded, and even if *he* knew he wasn't following through with that threat, she didn't.

He nearly laughed out loud at the image of her sputtering and gesticulating the day of their accident. Okay, *incident*. She wasn't likely to forgive him for making such a fuss over that fender-bender.

He collected the eggs and returned to the house. With an efficiency born of long practice, he scrambled half a dozen eggs, fried bacon and made toast. In the middle of his domestic efforts, Tom came in. They sat down to breakfast, exchanging a few words as they listened to the radio news, then headed out.

The morning sped by, and they finished the worming by eleven o'clock. Lonny drove into Red Springs to do errands; normally Tom liked to join him, but he'd been keeping to himself lately. During the past few days, he'd seemed more reserved than usual. Whatever the problem, the boy chose not to divulge it, which was fine. If and when he wanted to talk, Lonny was willing to listen.

Tom didn't have much to say at the best of times. The kid put in a good day's work, and that was all Lonny could expect. If Tom preferred to stay at the ranch, that was his business. Come to think of it, though, Tom had been mighty eager to get into town every chance he got—until recently. Lonny suspected Michelle Larson at the feed store had something to do with that. He couldn't help wondering what was going on there. It was probably as obvious as it seemed—a boy-girl thing. In that case, considering his own relationship difficulties, he wouldn't have much advice to offer.

As he drove toward town, Lonny turned the radio up as loud as he could stand it, listening to Johnny and

Willie and Garth, even singing along now and then. As he approached the intersection between Oak and Spruce, he remembered reading in the *Red Springs Journal* that the new stop sign had caused a couple of accidents in the past week. Real accidents, too, not just minor collisions. If this continued, the town was likely to order a traffic light. There was already one on Main Street, and in his opinion, one light was enough.

The first of his errands took him to the feed store. Lonny backed his pickup to the loading dock and tossed in a fifty-pound sack of chicken feed. The owner's daughter hurried out as soon as he pulled into the lot. When Michelle saw that he was alone, her face fell and she wandered back into the store.

Lonny paid for his purchase and stayed to have a cup of coffee with Charley Larson. They talked about the same things they always discussed. The weather, followed by the low price of cattle and the prospects for naturally raised beef. Then they rounded off their conversation with a discussion of the upcoming community carnival.

Lonny wasn't really surprised when Charley asked him, "What do you know about that hand you hired?"

"Tom?" Lonny said with a shrug. "Not much. He's of age, if that's what you're wondering. I checked, and as far as I can see, he's not in any trouble. He keeps to himself and he's a hard worker. What makes you ask?" Although Lonny could guess. . . .

Charley glanced over his shoulder toward the store. "My Michelle likes him."

"That bother you?"

"Not in the least," Charley muttered. "I think Michelle might've asked him to the school dance. He seems to have turned her down."

So *that* was the reason Tom was so gloomy these days. Lonny couldn't imagine why he'd said no to Michelle when he was so obviously taken with the girl. Apparently his hired hand was as inept at relationships as Lonny was himself. Granted, he'd never had any difficulties during his rodeo days, but Joy Fuller was a different proposition altogether. "I'll ask Tom about it and get back to you."

Charley hesitated. "If you do, be subtle about it, okay? Otherwise, Michelle will get upset with me."

"I will," Lonny promised, considering his options.

There was the school carnival, for starters. Lonny figured he'd go around suppertime—and while he was at it, he'd bring Tom. The dance was later that night, so if Tom was already in town, he'd have no excuse not to attend. These events weren't for another two weeks, but his sister had roped him into volunteering for the clean-up committee, which meant he'd be picking up trash and sweeping the street. She'd said something about him frying burgers with Chase, too. There was no point in arguing with her. Besides, he enjoyed the festivities.

Last year Joy had been working the cotton candy machine. He'd hoped to have a conversation with her, but he hadn't done it. For one thing, she'd been constantly busy, chatting with a crowd of people who all seemed to like her and have lots to say. For another, he'd felt uncharacteristically tongue-tied around her. He sure didn't want a bunch of interested onlookers witnessing his stumbling, fumbling attempts at conversation.

When he'd finished talking to Charley and climbed into the cab of his pickup, Lonny noticed a flash of green outside the town's biggest grocery store, situated across the street.

Lonny's eyes locked on Joy Fuller's green PT Cruiser. She pulled into the lot, parked and then headed into the store.

Groceries were on Lonny's list of errands. Nothing much, just the basics. Unexpectedly, the same happy feeling he'd experienced while driving into town with the radio blasting came over him. A carefree, what-the-hell feeling . . .

Lonny parked and jumped out of his pickup. His steps were light as he entered the store and grabbed a cart. His first stop was the vegetable aisle. It was too soon to expect much produce from Letty's garden. Last year, she'd seen to it that he got healthy portions of lettuce, green beans, fresh peas and zucchini. He was counting on her to do the same this summer. Until then, he had no choice but to buy a few vegetables himself.

Glancing around, he was disappointed not to see Joy. He tossed a bag of carrots in his cart, then threw in some lettuce and made his way to the meat department. She wasn't there. So he wheeled his cart to the back of the store, to the dairy case. He'd heard that a lot of women ate yogurt. But Joy wasn't in that section, either.

Then he heard her laugh.

Lonny smiled. The sound came from somewhere in the middle of the store. Turning his cart around, he trotted toward the frozen food. He should've known that was where he'd find her.

Here was proof that, unlike Letty, who cooked for her family, Joy didn't take much time to prepare meals. Neither did he, come to think of it—breakfast was his one and only specialty—which was why dinner invitations from Letty were appreciated. Tom and Lonny mostly fended for themselves. A can of soup or chili, a sandwich or two, was about as fancy as either of them got.

Sure enough, the instant Lonny turned into the aisle, he saw Joy. Her back was to him, and the three Wilson kids were chatting with her, along with their mom, Della. Lonny had gone to school with Della Harrison; she'd married Bobby Wilson, a friend of his, and had three kids in quick succession. Lonny didn't know whether to envy Bobby and Della or pity them.

He strolled up to the two women. "Hi, Della," he said, trying to seem casual and nonchalant. He nodded politely in Joy's direction and touched the brim of his Stetson.

The smile faded from Joy's face. "Mr. Ellison," she returned primly.

Lonny had trouble keeping his eyes off Joy. He had to admit she looked mighty fine in a pair of jeans. Both women gazed at him expectantly, and he didn't have a clue what to say next. Judging by her expression, Joy would rather be just about anywhere else at that moment.

"Good to run into you, Lonny," Della said pleasantly. "Bobby was saying the other day that we don't see near enough of you."

"Yeah, we'll get together soon." Lonny manufactured an anxious frown. "But I've been having problems with my truck. I had an accident recently and, well, it hasn't run the same since."

"Really?" Della asked.

"That's right," he said, wondering if he'd overdone the facade of wounded innocence.

"Miss Fuller is my teacher," a sweet little girl announced proudly.

Della was looking suspiciously from him to Joy. Lonny decided that was his cue to move on, and he would have, except that he made the mistake of glancing into Joy's grocery cart. It was just as he'd expected—frozen entrées. Only she'd picked the diet ones. She didn't need to be on any diet. In fact, her figure was about as perfect as a woman's could get. No wonder she'd snapped at him and been so irritable. The woman was starving herself.

"That's what you intend to eat this week?" he asked, reaching for one of the entrées. He felt suddenly hopeful. If she was hungry, the way he suspected, then she might accept an invitation to dinner. They could talk everything out over enchiladas and maybe a

Corona or two. Everything always seemed better on a full stomach.

"What's wrong with that?" she demanded, yanking the frozen entrée out of his hand and tossing it back in her cart.

"You shouldn't be on a diet," he insisted. "If that's what you're having for dinner, it's no wonder you're so skinny—or so mad."

"Lonny," Della gasped.

Oh, boy, he'd done it again. That comment hadn't come out quite as he'd intended. "I—you . . . I—" He tried to backtrack, but all he could manage was a bad imitation of a trout. As usual, his mouth had operated independently of his brain.

He turned to Della, but she glared at him with the same intensity as Joy. Instinct told him to hightail it out of the store before he made the situation worse than it already was.

"I didn't mean that like it sounded," he muttered. "You look fine for being underweight." Again he glanced at Della for help, but none was forthcoming. "You're a little on the thin side, that's all. Not much, of course. In fact, you're just about right."

"It's a male problem," Della said, speaking to Joy. She scowled. "They don't know when to keep their mouths shut."

"Uh, it was nice seeing you both," he said. He'd thought he was complimenting her, but to his utter astonishment, Joy's eyes had filled with tears.

Lonny's gut twisted. He couldn't imagine what he'd

said that was bad enough to make her cry. "Joy, I . . ."

Della looked at him with open contempt. He swallowed, not knowing how to fix this mess. He was aghast as Joy abruptly left the aisle, her grocery cart rattling.

"See what you've done?" Della hissed at him beneath her breath. "You idiot."

"What's wrong with Miss Fuller?" the little girl asked. "What did that man do?" She focused her blue eyes on him and had he been a lesser man, Lonny would've backed off. If looks could kill, his sister would be planning his burial service about now.

"I—I didn't mean anything," Lonny stammered, feeling as low as a man could get.

"You're hopeless," Della said, shaking her head.

The girl shook her head, too, eyes narrowed. The kid came by that evil look naturally, Lonny realized.

"I . . . I . . ."

"The least you can do is apologize." Della's fingers gripped the cart handle.

"I tried." He motioned helplessly.

"You didn't try hard enough." With that Della sped away, her children in tow. The little girl marched to the end of the aisle, then turned back and stuck out her tongue at him.

A sick feeling attacked the pit of his stomach. He should've known better. He'd already decided not to pursue a relationship with Joy and then, next thing he knew, he was inviting her for dinner. A lot of good *that* had done him.

He felt dreadful, worse than dreadful. He'd actually made Joy cry, but God's honest truth, he couldn't believe a little comment like that was worthy of tears.

He walked up to the front of the store only to see Joy dash out, carrying two grocery bags. Abandoning his cart, he hurried after her.

"Joy," he called, sprinting into the parking lot.

At the sound of his voice she whirled around and confronted him. "In case you hadn't already guessed, I'm not interested in speaking to you."

"I—ah . . ." In his entire life, Lonny had never backed down from a confrontation. Served him right that the first time it happened would be with a woman.

"You were trying to embarrass me. Trying to make me feel stupid."

"I . . . I—" For some reason, he couldn't make his tongue form the words in his brain.

"You poked fun at me, called me skinny. Well, maybe I am, but—"

"You aren't," he cried. "I just said that because . . . because it didn't look like you were eating enough and I thought maybe I could feed you."

"Feed me?"

"Dinner."

"Just leave me alone!" Joy left him and bolted for her car.

Lonny exhaled sharply. Following her was probably a bad idea—another one in a long list of them. He would've preferred to simply go home, but he couldn't make himself do it. Unable to come up with any alternative, Lonny jogged after her. He wouldn't sleep tonight if he didn't tell her how sorry he was.

He knew she'd heard his footsteps, because the instant she set the groceries in the Cruiser's trunk, she whirled around. They were practically nose to nose. "I don't need you to feed me or talk to me or anything else," she said. "All I want you to do is *leave me alone.*"

"I will, only you have to listen to me first." Damn, this was hard. "I didn't mean to suggest you were unattractive, because you are."

"Unattractive?" she cried. "I'm *unattractive?* This is supposed to be an apology? Is that why you decided not to see me two years ago? You thought I was too skinny?"

"No, no, I meant you're attractive." Could this possibly get any worse? "Anyway, that has nothing to do with now. Can't you just accept my apology? Are you always this hotheaded?"

Eyes glistening, she turned and slammed the trunk lid. The noise reverberated around the parking lot.

Nothing he said was going to help; the situation seemed completely out of his control. "I think you're about as beautiful as a girl can get." There, he'd said it.

She stared at him for a long moment. "What did you say?"

"You're beautiful," he repeated. He hadn't intended to tell her that, even if it was true. Which it was.

The fire in her eyes gradually died away, replaced by a quizzical look that said she wasn't sure she could believe him. But then she smiled.

Lonny felt a burst of sheer happiness at that smile.

She glanced down at the asphalt. "When I was growing up, I had knobby knees and skinny legs and I was teased unmercifully. The other kids used to call me Skel. Short for skeleton."

That explained a lot.

"I had no idea."

"You couldn't have," she assured him. "When you said I was skinny, it brought back a lot of bad memories."

In an effort to comfort her, Lonny pulled her close. That was when insanity took over for the second time that day. Even knowing they were in the middle of town in the grocery-store parking lot, even knowing she'd told him in no uncertain terms to leave her alone, Lonny bent forward and kissed her.

Kissing Joy felt good. She seemed to be experiencing the same wonderful sensation, because she didn't object. He knew he was right when she wound her arms around his neck and she opened to him, as naturally as could be.

Lonny groaned. They kissed with a passion that was as heated as any argument they'd ever had. He wanted to tell her again how sorry he was, how deeply he regretted everything he'd said, and he prayed his kisses were enough to convey what was in his heart.

Then all at once Joy's hands were pushing him away. Caught off guard, Lonny stumbled back. He would've landed squarely on his butt if not for some quick shuffling.

"What did you do *that* for?" She brought one hand to her mouth.

"I don't know," he admitted quietly. "I wanted to tell you I was sorry, and that seemed as good a way as any."

She backed toward the driver's door as if she didn't trust him not to reach for her a second time.

He might have, too, if he'd felt he had the slightest chance of reasoning with her—or resuming their previous activity.

"Well, don't do it again."

"Fine," he said. She made it sound as if that kiss had been against her will. Not so. She could deny it, but he knew the truth. Joy Fuller had wanted that kiss as much as he had.

Chapter Six

Joy couldn't figure out how that kiss had ever happened. As she drove home, she touched her finger to her swollen lips. What shocked her most was how much she'd *enjoyed* his kiss. They'd kissed before, back in their dating days, but it certainly hadn't affected her like this. Her irritation rose. Lonny Ellison had insulted her, and in response, she'd let him *kiss* her?

Upset as she was, Joy nearly ran through the stop sign at Spruce and Oak. Again. She slammed on her brakes hard, which jolted her forward with enough force to lock her seat belt so tightly she could barely breathe.

Just as quickly, she was thrown back against the seat. When she did manage to catch her breath, she exhaled shakily as her pulse hammered in her ears.

Once she got home, Joy unpacked her groceries and tried hard to put that ridiculous kiss out of her mind. The fact that Lonny had apologized was a lame excuse for what he'd done—and she'd allowed. Standing in her kitchen, Joy covered her face with both hands. For heaven's sake, they'd been in a parking lot! Anyone driving by or coming out of the store might have witnessed that . . . that torrid scene.

Her face burned at the mere thought of it. She'd worked hard to maintain a solid reputation in the community, and now Lonny Ellison and her own reckless behavior threatened to destroy it.

Thankfully, her afternoon was busy; otherwise she would've spent the rest of the day worrying. She had choir practice at two o'clock at the church and there was a Carnival Committee meeting at school immediately following that. Joy's one desperate hope was that no one she knew had been anywhere near the grocery store this morning.

By the time she arrived at the church, her stomach was in turmoil. As she took her place at the organ, she surreptitiously watched the choir members. Fortunately, no one seemed to pay her any particular attention. That was promising, although she supposed the last person they'd say anything to would be her. Once she was out of sight, the gossip would probably spread faster than an August brushfire.

To her relief, practice went well. Joy stayed on when everyone had left and played through the songs, which helped settle her nerves. Music had always had a calming effect on her, and that was exactly what she needed.

Kissing in public. Dear heaven, what was she thinking? Of course, that was the problem. She *hadn't* been thinking. All reason had flown from her brain. But regardless of her own role in this, she cast the greater part of the blame at Lonny Ellison's feet. His sole purpose in commenting on her diet had been to embarrass her.

At three, the school parking lot started to fill up for the meeting. The committees had been formed months earlier, and their main purpose now was to raise funds in order to finance the end-of-school carnival. Bringing in professional carnival rides had put a definite strain on their limited budget. But everyone in town was excited about it, and the committee would do whatever was necessary to finance the rides, for which they planned to charge only a nominal fee.

A number of women had already gathered in the high school gymnasium when Joy slipped into the meeting. She sat in the back row, where she was soon joined by Letty Brown. Involuntarily, Joy tensed, afraid Lonny might have mentioned their kiss to his sister. Apparently not, because Letty smiled at her, and they made small talk for several minutes. That didn't prove anything, though.

"When's the last time you talked to your brother?"

Joy asked when she couldn't stand the suspense anymore.

Letty frowned. "A couple of days ago. Why?"

It demanded all of Joy's acting skills to give a nonchalant shrug. "No reason."

A moment later, Doris Fleming banged the gavel to bring the meeting to order. After the preliminaries and the reading of the minutes, Doris announced, "I have all the game prizes ordered, I've paid for the carnival, and—I'm shocked to tell you—our finances have been entirely depleted. We need to raise funds and we need to do it fast, otherwise we'll have no operating budget. We still have to buy food, drinks and so forth."

Janice Rothchild's hand shot into the air. "We could do a bake sale. That's always good for raising money."

A few women groaned. Muttering broke out until Doris banged the gavel again.

"A bake sale's always been our best money-raiser," Janice reminded the other women. She should know because she'd been the carnival treasurer for as long as Joy had been in town.

"Well, yes, Della's pies sell out right away, and Florence Williams's sourdough biscuits, too, of course."

"Don't forget Sally's chocolate cake," Myrtle Jameson shouted out. "That's one of the first to go. But last year, *everything* was sold out in under two hours."

"Order, please," Doris said. She held her index finger to her lips. "Myrtle, you're right. Remember how, at the last bake sale, there was a line outside the door even before we opened? And Betty," she said, pointing her gavel at a woman who sat in the front row. "Tell the ladies what happened to you."

Betty Sanders, who was well into her eighties, stood, using her cane for balance. "One of the men stopped me in the parking lot and bought all my butterhorn rolls the second I got out of my car."

"See what I mean?" Janice said, looking around for confirmation. "That's why I suggested we do a bake sale. They're *very* popular."

"I have another idea," Letty said, leaping to her feet. The women twisted around to see who was speaking. "If the bake sale's so popular and we sell out right away, why don't we auction off the baked goods?"

Letty sat back down and the room instantly erupted into discordant chatter.

Doris pounded the gavel and Joy could see that she was keen on Letty's idea.

"That's a fabulous suggestion," Doris said. "We'd raise a lot more cash—and our treasury could sure use it."

"But where would we hold an auction?" someone called out. "Especially at this late date? Don't forget, the carnival's only two weeks away."

A variety of suggestions followed. Finally someone else brought forth the idea of having the auction during Friday-night bingo at the community center. Expressions of approval rippled across the room.

"An auction's a perfect idea." Joy leaned close in order to whisper to her friend.

"I don't know why someone hasn't thought of it

before," Letty said, shrugging off the praise.

"Bingo is the most popular event of the week," Lois Franklin reminded the group. "And Bill told me he always needs entertainment for intermission. I know he'll welcome this idea."

"It helps that you're married to him, too," Doris said, chuckling. "So we can count on holding the auction at bingo?"

Lois nodded. "I'll personally make sure of it."

"It's as good as done, then," Doris said. "Thank you, Lois."

"When?" another woman asked. "Next Friday?"

Doris glanced around. "Does a week give everyone enough time to get the word out?"

There were nods of assent.

Although she'd hoped to remain inconspicuous during this meeting, Joy didn't feel she could keep silent. She raised her hand and stood. "That only gives us seven days—including today—to let people know." They'd need to have signs made and posted around town right away.

After another round of muttered rumblings, Doris slammed the gavel yet again. "That's true, but there's nothing we can do about it. The bake sale auction is set for next Friday night."

"We'll tell everyone," Betty said, leaning on her cane.

"No problem." Honey Sue Jameson got to her feet. "I'll make it my business to tell the entire town about this." Honey Sue was Myrtle's daughter-in-law. She and her husband, Don, owned the local radio station, so she was on the radio every morning, announcing the news and reading the farm report. Honey Sue had come by her name because her voice was as sweet and smooth as honey. Although Joy had no interest in the price of beef or soybeans, she sometimes tuned in just to hear Honey Sue. She could actually make a list of prices sound almost poetic.

"That's terrific," Doris said, beaming at the prospect of filling the committee's coffers. "I'll put out sheets of paper for sign-up lists. Ladies, please indicate what you're bringing and how you can help publicize our bake sale."

"Just a minute," Betty said, returning everyone's attention to the front of the room. "Who'll be the auctioneer?"

"We could always ask Don," Lois Franklin suggested.

"If he won't do it, I will," Honey Sue volunteered.

Once again Doris nodded her approval.

"Will the name of whoever contributed the baked item be mentioned?" someone else wanted to know.

Doris frowned. "I . . ." She looked to Honey Sue for advice. "What do you think?"

Honey Sue smiled. "I don't suppose it could hurt."

"The name of the donor will be announced at the time the baked item is brought up for auction," Doris stated decisively.

"That might generate even higher bids," Letty murmured. "Chase is crazy for Betty's butterhorn rolls. He doesn't know it, but Betty gave me the recipe. I just haven't gotten around to baking them yet."

Joy whispered in Letty's ear. "So it was Chase who stopped her in the parking lot?"

"I'm not sure, but knowing Chase, it probably was."

Several sheets of paper were set up on the front table, and the women stepped forward to write down their donations.

Joy and Letty joined the line. "What are you going to bake?" Joy asked her friend.

"Pecan pie," Letty said without hesitation. "What about you?"

Several ideas ran through Joy's mind. No doubt Lonny thought she purchased frozen entrées because she didn't know how to cook. Well, that wasn't the case. She should arrive with Cherries Jubilee, toss on the brandy and light it up. She could just imagine Lonny Ellison's expression when he saw flames leaping into the air. Or perhaps Baked Alaska. That would make a point, too.

"I haven't decided yet," she murmured.

"Remember that day you watched Cricket for me?" Letty said. "The two of you baked peanut butter cookies. They were wonderful."

"You think so?" Joy didn't mean to sound so insecure. The cookies were fine, but they didn't provide the dramatic statement she was hoping to make. She shouldn't worry about impressing anyone, least of all Lonny. Still, the thought flitted through her mind. She would derive great satisfaction from seeing his face when she presented Crêpes Suzette.

Joy didn't have a single thing to prove to Lonny, or anyone else for that matter, and yet she *wanted* to impress him. It was all about pride. This . . . this cowpoke was taking up far too much of her time and energy. She didn't want to be attracted to him. Josh was coming back into her life and he was someone she knew, someone she felt comfortable with. Lonny made her angry every time she thought about him, he'd embarrassed her publicly more than once, *and* they had absolutely nothing in common.

"Cricket loves to bake now," Letty continued, "and it all comes from that afternoon with you."

"Peanut butter cookies are so . . ." Joy paused, searching for the right word. "*Ordinary,*" she finished.

Letty grinned. "In case you haven't noticed, most everyone around these parts prefers ordinary. We're a meat-and-potatoes kind of community. You won't see anyone signing up to bring Crêpes Suzette."

"Ah . . ." So much for that idea.

"It's a lesson I learned when I came back after living in California all those years," Letty went on. "I didn't need to impress anyone. All I had to do was be myself."

Even though Joy longed to see the look on Lonny's face when the auctioneer brought forth her fabulously exclusive dessert and read her name, she realized she'd only embarrass herself. No one would bid on it; no doubt they'd feel sorry for her, the city girl who'd tried to show off her superior baking skills.

"Peanut butter cookies it is," she said with a sigh.

Letty reached the front of the line and wrote down

pecan pie. Joy added her cookies to the list, noticing that only one other woman had offered to bake them.

Letty waited for her, and together they walked to the parking lot. Several other cars were pulling out.

"Is something going on between my brother and you?" Letty asked unexpectedly.

Joy almost couldn't swallow her gasp of alarm. "W-what do you mean?"

"Well, you *did* ask about him," Letty said. "You wanted to know if I'd talked to my brother recently."

"Oh, that." Joy brushed off the question. "No reason." It was the same response she'd made earlier, but she couldn't come up with a more inventive excuse on the spur of the moment.

Letty regarded her as if she knew there *was* a reason. "Well, regardless, we'll see him soon enough."

"We will?" Joy widened her eyes. She'd sincerely hoped to avoid him.

"Of course," Letty said matter-of-factly. "You can bet he'll be at the auction." And with that simple statement, she both confirmed Joy's fears and ignited her hopes.

Chapter Seven

Lonny had plenty to do around the ranch. Early in the afternoon, after he got back from town, he rode out to the herd, seeking any cattle that showed signs of sickness. Chase had found one heifer with a runny nose and isolated her for the time being.

Lonny felt a sense of pride as his gaze fell on the rows of wheat, stretching as far as the eye could see. The stalks were still slender and light green. He and Chase had planted three hundred acres, another three hundred in soybeans and nearly that much in natural grasses. The wheat was grown for grazing and for seed. They grew everything their cattle ate. The herd now numbered about four hundred, and their goal was to eventually increase it to fifteen hundred head.

A herd that size would take years to develop, depending on the public's response to natural beef. He had to believe that once health-conscious consumers realized they had a choice, they'd prefer a product devoid of potentially harmful chemicals. Both Chase and Lonny had staked their financial future on this hope.

Thinking about their plans for the herd distracted him from Joy Fuller—but not for long. Following that scene this morning, he was half afraid his sister might be right. He *was* attracted to Joy. He had been earlier, too, when they'd first dated, only it had all blown up in his face. The woman was opinionated and argumentative—but then, so was he. Together, they were like a match striking tinder. Saturday's kiss had showed him how quickly that could lead to combustion.

He understood now why he'd reacted so irrationally at the time of the accident. He knew why he'd insisted she take responsibility for the damage to his truck. The truth had hit him squarely between the eyes when he kissed her. It shook him, mainly because he didn't *want* to be attracted to Joy. They'd already tried a relationship and he'd decided it just wasn't going to work. It wouldn't this time, either, and now . . . now, he thought, looking over the cattle scattered across the green land, he had other considerations, other worries.

Tom came into view on Dolly, the brown-and-white mare he preferred to ride. He was unusually mature for nineteen and, to Lonny's relief, didn't require much supervision. He gave Tom a few instructions, then rode back to the barn. He should check the fence line, which needed continual attention. Yet whenever he started a task, he had to struggle not to get sidetracked by thoughts of Joy . . . and that kiss.

Twice he'd actually climbed inside his truck, intending to go into town so he could talk to her. He didn't know what he could possibly say that would make a shred of difference. He was convinced that she'd enjoyed their kiss as much as he had, but she'd insisted she didn't want him touching her.

For a moment there, for one of the most wonderful interludes of his life, she'd kissed him back. Then she'd suddenly broken it off.

Once he'd finished rubbing down his horse, Lonny walked resolutely toward the truck. He would go to Joy, he decided, take his hat off and ask if they could talk man to man—no, that wouldn't work. Man to woman, then. They'd clear up past misunderstandings and perhaps they could start fresh.

He'd apologize, too, for the way he'd behaved after the accident, and tell her she didn't need to pay him a dime to repair that dent. It added character, he'd say. He wouldn't mention their kiss, though. If he apologized, he'd be lying and she'd see right through him.

Determined now, even though it was already late afternoon, he climbed into his truck. It was at this point that he'd changed his mind twice before. Based on his frustrating inability to forget about Joy for more than a few minutes, he could only conclude that it wouldn't do him any good to stick around the ranch. In his current emotional state, he wasn't worth a plugged nickel, anyway.

The twenty-minute drive into town seemed to pass in five. Before he had a chance to think about what he intended to say, he'd reached Joy's house. At least he assumed she still lived in the same duplex she'd rented when she moved to town. He parked outside and clutched the steering wheel for probably three minutes before he found the gumption to walk to the front door. Checking the contents of the mailbox confirmed that this was, indeed, her home.

Lonny wasn't fond of eating crow and he was about to swallow a sizable portion. He was willing to do it, though, if that would set things straight between him and Joy.

Squaring his shoulders, he cleared his throat and removed his Stetson. He shook his head in case his hair was flat, took a deep breath and braced his feet apart. Then he rang her doorbell.

Nothing.

He pressed it again, harder and longer this time.

Still nothing.

Lonny peeked in the front window. There didn't appear to be anyone home. Now that he thought about it, her little green PT Cruiser was nowhere in sight.

Disappointed, Lonny went back to his own vehicle. It seemed important to let her know he'd made an effort to contact her. Digging around in his glove compartment, he found a slip of paper—an old gas station receipt— and a pencil stub. He spent a moment thinking about what to say. After careful consideration, he wrote: *I came to talk. I think we should, don't you? Call me. Lonny J. Ellison.* Then he wrote down his phone number.

He'd added his middle initial so she'd realize he was serious. His father had chosen Jethro as his middle name, and he usually avoided any reminder of it. For Joy, he'd reveal his embarrassing secret—because if she asked what the J stood for, he'd tell her.

As he pulled away from the curb and turned the corner, he glanced in his rearview mirror and saw her green car coming from the opposite direction.

Lonny made a quick U-turn and parked just out of sight. Leaning over his steering wheel, he managed to get a glimpse of Joy's front porch. Sure enough, it was her.

His best course of action, he decided, was to wait and see what happened when she found his note.

Lonny watched Joy walk slowly toward the house. He noticed that her shoulders were hunched as if she wasn't feeling well. She opened the screen door and the slip of paper he'd tucked there dropped to the porch.

Lonny almost called out, afraid she hadn't seen it. She had, though. Bending down, she picked up the note he'd folded in half. He held his breath as she read it. Then he saw her take his heartfelt message, crumple it with both hands and shove it inside her pocket. After that, she unlocked the front door, slammed it shut and drew her drapes.

Lonny sighed. Perhaps now wasn't a good time to approach her, after all.

On the drive back to his ranch, Lonny wondered how his plan could have gone so wrong. Joy's reaction to his note made it clear that she wasn't interested in anything he had to say. He could take a hint. But in his opinion, she wasn't being honest with herself; otherwise, she would've acknowledged how much she'd liked that kiss. Fine. He could deal with it.

The rest of the day was shot, so Lonny stopped at Chase and Letty's. As soon as his truck rolled into the yard, Cricket came running out of the house, bouncing down the porch steps.

Lonny was out of his vehicle just in time to catch her in his arms and swing her around. Now, *this* was a gratifying reception—exactly the type he'd hoped to get from Joy. That, however, was not to be, and he assured himself that he'd dismissed the notion.

"Mom's baking pecan pie," Cricket announced.

"For dinner?" he asked, setting his niece down on the ground.

Cricket frowned. "I don't think so."

"Your mommy makes the best pecan pie I ever tasted." If he hung around a while, she might offer him a piece.

Chase stepped out of the barn, wiping his brow with his forearm. "What are you doing here?" he asked. "I thought you were going to finish the worming."

"Good to see you, too," Lonny teased. They'd been best friends their entire lives. Friends, partners, neighbors—and now, brothers-in-law. "Tom and I finished the worming early this morning." Early enough to race into town and make an idiot of himself over Joy. That, however, was information he planned to keep private.

"Aren't you and Tom driving the herd to the lower pasture this weekend?"

"I decided against it," Lonny said. "There's still plenty of grass in the upper pasture. I meant to tell you. . . ."

Letty came out onto the back porch and waved when she saw him. "Hi, Lonny," she said. She didn't look as if she'd been baking.

"What's this I hear about a pecan pie?" he asked, moving closer. If he was lucky, she'd offer him a piece *and* invite him to dinner. In that case, he'd casually bring up the subject of Joy and get his sister's opinion. Maybe he needed a woman's perspective.

"I'm not baking the pie until later in the week. It's for an auction. Want to stay for dinner? I'm just setting the table."

"What're you making?"

"Roast chicken, scalloped potatoes, green bean casserole."

He grinned. "It'd be my pleasure." Letty's cooking was downright inspired, and this meal reminded him of one their mother might have made. Toward the end of her life, though, she'd taken more interest in painting landscapes than in the culinary arts. Letty had inherited their mother's abilities in the kitchen, and she could do artistic stuff, too—knitting and flower arranging and other things, like the dried herb wreath that hung on the kitchen door.

"I'll wash up and join you in a few minutes," Chase said.

"Cricket, go add another place setting to the table," Letty instructed her daughter.

"Can Uncle Lonny sit next to me?"

"I wouldn't sit anywhere else," Lonny said as the six-year-old followed her mother up the steps.

"Were you in town today?" Letty asked.

Lonny paused, unsure how much to tell his sister. "I just made a quick trip," he said cautiously. He'd actually made two trips, but he didn't point *that* out.

"Did you happen to run into Joy?"

He froze in midstep. "Why do you ask?"

Letty eyed him speculatively. "What is it with you two?" she demanded, hands on hips. "I asked Joy about you and she clammed right up."

"Really?" Lonny played it cool. If she wasn't talking, then he wasn't, either. He didn't know how many people had caught sight of the spectacle they'd

made of themselves—and whether someone had tat-
tled to Letty.

"I wish you and Joy would talk," she said, in the same
sisterly tone she'd used when they were kids. "It's
ridiculous the way you keep circling each other. *One* of
you needs to be adult enough to discuss this."

"I agree with you." His response seemed to surprise
her. What Letty didn't know was that Lonny had
already tried, and it hadn't gotten him anywhere. He
held open the screen door. "It's obvious," he said,
tossing Letty a cocky smile. "The woman wants me."

"The only thing that's obvious to me, big brother, is
that you're so in love with her you can't think straight."

He laughed that off—but he was man enough to
admit there was *something* between him and Joy.
However, exactly what it was and how deep it went,
not to mention how he should handle it, remained a
mystery.

Letty walked into the kitchen and poured him a cup
of coffee. "You tried talking to her?"

Lonny took the mug and shook his head. He hadn't
spoken to Joy, not technically; he'd left her a note.
Rather than explain, he didn't answer the question.
"Tell me about the auction. What's it for?"

Letty studied him as he added sugar to his coffee. "I
signed up to bring a pecan pie for a bake sale auction.
The carnival committee needs operating capital, and we
need to raise it quickly."

"You aren't going to sell the goodies the way you normally do?" That was a disappointment. An auction

would drive up the prices. Lonny had a sweet tooth and he was generally first in line for a bake sale. This pie might prove to be expensive.

"If you want the pecan pie, you're going to have to bid on it like everyone else," his sister gleefully informed him. "Otherwise, you'll have to wait until next Thanksgiving."

Head down, Lonny muttered a few words he didn't want Cricket or his sister to hear.

"I was at a meeting about the bake sale this afternoon," Letty said as he leaned his hip against the kitchen counter. "Joy was there, too."

That remark captured his attention; Lonny suddenly lifted his head and realized his little sister had just baited him. He'd fallen for it, too, hook, line and sinker. In an effort to cover his interest, he laughed. "You're telling me Joy's contributing to the bake sale?" Apparently his sister was unaware that the woman's meals came from the freezer section of the grocery store.

His sister didn't see the humor in it, so he felt he needed to enlighten her. "Do you seriously think she can bake?"

"Why not?" Letty asked, eyebrows raised.

Lonny could see he was getting more involved in the subject than was really prudent. He considered telling Letty about seeing Joy earlier, then promptly decided against it. With a quick shrug, he said, "Oh, nothing."

Lonny wondered what was taking Chase so long to wash up. He could use a diversion. Sighing, he thought he might as well get Letty's advice now. The hell with being sensible or discreet. "I blew it with Joy," he said in a low voice.

His confession didn't come easy. Before he could think better of it, Lonny described the incident inside the store, stopping short of the kiss. It wasn't that he was opposed to telling his family the full truth—eventually. Cricket excepted, of course. If he and Joy had been seen, the gossip would find its way to Letty soon enough; in fact, he was surprised she hadn't heard anything yet. But that kiss was special. For as long as possible, he wanted to keep those moments to himself.

"You said *what?*" his sister exploded after listening to the whole sad story.

Lonny pulled out a chair and sat down. "I feel bad about it now. She said she got teased about being thin as a kid, and I stepped in it with both feet."

"Lonny!"

It didn't help having his sister yell at him. He knew he'd made a mistake; she didn't need to beat up on him all over again. Della and her daughters had done an adequate job of that already.

"I apologized," he muttered, rubbing his hands over his eyes. "Well, I tried."

Letty frowned.

"What?" he snapped. If Chase didn't arrive soon, he'd go and search for the guy himself.

"This is what you're going to do," his sister said, speaking slowly and clearly, as though he were hard of hearing—or deficient in understanding.

"Now, Letty . . ."

"You're going to bid on Joy's peanut butter cookies." His sister wouldn't allow him to interrupt. Letty was still frowning, her eyes narrowed. "And you're going to be the highest bidder."

"Okay." That much he could do.

She nodded, evidently approving his willingness to fall in with her scheme. Well, he supposed she couldn't get him into worse trouble with Joy than he was now.

"And then," Letty continued, "you're going to *taste* Joy's cookies and declare these are the best you've ever had in your entire life."

"I am?" This seemed a little overboard to Lonny.

"Yes, you will, and you're going to mean it, too."

Lonny wasn't so sure about that, but he'd hear his sister out. He'd asked for her opinion, and the least he could do was listen.

Fortunately, Chase clattered down the stairs at that moment, putting a temporary end to Letty's career as a romantic advisor.

Chapter Eight

Wednesday afternoon Joy hurried home from school, planning to do some baking. She'd spent far too much time reading through cookbooks and searching various Web sites on the Internet, looking for a spectacular dessert that would wow the boots off a certain rancher.

Every time she found a recipe she was sure would impress Lonny, Joy remembered the scorn in his eyes when he'd picked up her frozen dinner. He'd probably fall over in a dead faint when he realized that not only could she bake, she was good at it.

Since she'd wasted so many hours on research, Joy had yet to make her peanut butter cookies, a recipe handed down from her grandmother. This recipe was an old family favorite.

She turned on the radio and arranged her ingredients. Flour, sugar, peanut butter . . . She lined them up along the counter in order of use. Bowls, measuring cups and utensils waited on the kitchen table; the oven was preheating and the cookie sheet greased. She was nothing if not organized.

The doorbell rang just as she was measuring the flour. Joy set the bag down and hurried into the front hall, curious to find out who her visitor might be.

Letty stood there, with Cricket at her side, and Joy immediately opened the screen door. "Come in," she said, glad of the company.

"Thanks," Letty said, smiling as she stepped into the house. "I was in town to buy pecans and thought I'd come over and see how you're doing."

"I'm baking," Joy announced. "Or at least, I'm getting started."

Letty hesitated. "I don't want to interrupt. . . ."

"I haven't actually begun, so your timing's perfect," she said, ushering Letty and Cricket into the kitchen.

"Can I play on your computer?" Cricket asked when her mother sat down at the table.

Joy glanced at Letty, who nodded, and Cricket loped

eagerly toward the spare bedroom. Apparently, Chase had taught her solitaire.

With a sweep of her hand, Letty indicated the half-dozen cookbooks Joy had spread out on the table and on two of her four chairs. In addition, she had a six-inch stack of recipes she'd printed off the Internet.

"What's all this?" Letty asked, as Joy cleared a chair and sat down across from her.

"Dessert recipes," Joy admitted a bit sheepishly.

Letty reached for one on the stack she'd gotten off the Internet. "Cannoli?" she read, and Joy watched her friend's face as she scanned the directions. "This sounds complicated."

Joy had thought so herself. "I could probably manage it, but I was afraid I'd waste a lot of time shaping them and then I'd need to fill them, too. Besides, they're deep-fried and I don't know how well they'd keep."

"You said you were baking peanut butter cookies."

"I am," Joy was quick to tell her, motioning toward the counter, "but I also wanted to bring something more . . . impressive. I'm a good cook and . . ." She let the rest fade. Since Letty was Lonny's sister, she couldn't very well confess what she was trying to prove and why. The less Letty knew about her most recent encounter with Lonny, the better.

"Tiramisu?" Letty cocked her head as she read the recipe title in a cookbook that was open directly in front of her. She looked skeptical when she returned her attention to Joy.

"I rejected that one, too," Joy confessed. "I wasn't

sure I could get all the ingredients without having to drive into Red Rock or Cheyenne."

"Baklava?" Letty asked next, pointing at another recipe.

"I had no idea whether anyone in town would even know what that was," Joy said. "There isn't a large Greek population in the area, is there?"

"No." Letty confirmed what Joy already suspected.

"The Raspberry Truffle Torte Bombe had possibilities," Joy said, gesturing at yet another of the cookbooks. "However, I was afraid the ice cream would melt."

"Joy, what's wrong with peanut butter cookies?" Letty asked.

"Nothing. I just wanted to bake more than one thing."

"Then bake a cake, and not a chocolate truffle one, either," she said, reaching for another of the pages Joy had printed out. "Just a plain, simple cake. That'll generate more interest than anything with melting ice cream in the middle."

"It will?"

Letty nodded and seemed surprised that she had to remind Joy of the obvious. "You've been part of this community long enough to know this," she said mildly. "You don't need to impress anyone."

Least of all Lonny Ellison, Joy mused. "You're right," she agreed. Actually, she was relieved. Although she was willing to try, she wasn't convinced she could pull off a culinary masterpiece before Friday night. She was a little out of practice.

She shouldn't be thinking about Lonny at all. Josh would be here soon, and there'd be a chance to renew that relationship.

"You're bringing more than the pecan pie, though, aren't you?" Joy asked, determined not to think about either man.

Letty nodded. "Chase suggested I bake a Lemonade Cake, which is one of his favorites. I suspect he wants to bid on it himself." She smiled as she said it.

Joy envied Letty the warm, loving relationship she had with her husband. She couldn't imagine Chase saying or doing any of the things Lonny Ellison had said and done to her. More and more, she thought about their earlier relationship and how they'd walked away from each other after some ridiculous, forgettable argument. Maybe she was partly to blame. If she was honest, she'd have to admit there was no *maybe* about it. And, still being honest, she regretted the lost opportunity. But it was too late, especially with Josh showing up.

Letty and Chase shared a special love story, and now that they were married, it seemed as if they'd always been together. Chase had loved Letty from the time he was a teenager; in fact, he'd loved her enough to let her leave Wyoming without guilt so she could pursue her dream of becoming a singer. For ten years Letty had worked hard at creating a musical career, with moderate success, getting fairly steady gigs as a background singer and doing a few commercials that still paid residuals from time to time. When she returned to Wyoming, she came back with a daughter and a heart ailment that threatened to shorten her life. She'd been born with it but had never known there was any problem; it had been discovered during her pregnancy. In her own mind, she'd come home to die. But she'd had the required surgery and could live an almost normal life now.

"Other than cookies, what do you enjoy baking?" Letty asked.

Because she lived alone and generally cooked for one, Joy hadn't done much baking since her arrival in Red Springs. Before college, she used to spend hours in the kitchen, often with her mother. "My mom taught me a great apple pie recipe," Joy said after a moment.

"Then bake an apple pie."

Apple pie—it felt as if a weight had been lifted from Joy's shoulders. "That's what I'll do," she said triumphantly.

"My brother's got a real sweet tooth," Letty murmured.

Joy shrugged, implying that was of little concern to her. She supposed this was Letty's way of reminding her that Lonny would be attending the auction. Joy wasn't sure how to react.

Her feelings on the subject of Lonny were decidedly mixed, and no one else had ever had such a confusing effect on her. Joy genuinely liked all the people who were close to him—Letty, of course, and Chase who was Lonny's best friend. Not to mention Cricket, who talked nonstop about her wonderful Uncle Lonny. He was obviously popular with the other ranchers and townsfolk, too. In other words, no one except her seemed to have a problem with him.

She was tempted to ask Letty about it. She hesitated, unsure how to introduce her question, but before she could say anything, Letty said it was time she left.

"Thanks for coming over," Joy said as she walked Letty and Cricket to the front door.

"Bake that pie," Letty advised yet again. "*After* you make those cookies."

"I will," Joy promised.

"See you Friday night. Do you want Chase and me to pick you up?"

Joy shook her head. "Honey Sue called and asked me to help with the setup, so I'll need to be there early."

Letty nodded, and Joy was grateful she had an excuse for declining the ride. If Lonny came into town for the auction, he'd sit with the couple, and if she joined them, too, the situation might be awkward for everyone.

Joy didn't want to think about Lonny anymore, but it was hard to avoid. She'd found his message in her screen door on Saturday, after the carnival committee meeting. At the time she'd been so angry and upset, she'd tossed it without even considering his suggestion. But perhaps he was right. Perhaps it would be a good idea to clear the air. Then again, to what end? They'd already learned that their personalities and beliefs were diametrically opposed, and that wasn't likely to change. Besides, Josh was coming. No, she'd better forget about Lonny—once she'd demonstrated her culinary aptitude.

The evening news was on when Joy finished baking a double batch of the peanut butter cookies. This was a tried and true recipe, tested a million times over the years, and there was no question that these were some of her best. They came out of the oven looking perfect. Her grandmother had used fork tines to create a criss-cross pattern on each one, and Joy followed tradition. Once they'd cooled, she carefully arranged them in a couple of tin boxes left over from Christmas and stored them in the cupboard until Friday night.

Just as she was flipping through her family cookbook, searching for her grandmother's apple pie recipe, the phone rang. The interruption annoyed her. She'd been fantasizing about the bidding war over the cookies and the apple pie and was busy picturing Lonny's shocked face, an image she wanted to hold on to as long as she could.

"Hello," she answered on the third ring, hoping her frustration wasn't evident.

"Joy, it's Josh."

Caught up as she was in her dream world, it took her a moment to remember who Josh was.

"Josh! Hi," she said quickly.

"Am I calling at a bad time?"

"No, no, of course not." It wasn't as if she could admit she'd been obsessively thinking about another man.

"Is someone there?" Josh asked after a brief hesitation.

"No, what makes you ask?"

95

"You sound preoccupied."

"I'm in the middle of baking."

"You bake?" He asked this as if it were a big joke.

She sighed. Not another one. "Yes, I know how to bake." Joy was unable to keep the irritation out of her voice. "I didn't mean that the way it came across," she added hastily. "There's a bake sale auction in town this Friday and—well, never mind, it isn't important."

Those remarks were followed by a short pause. "Joy," he said solemnly, "are you involved with anyone?"

"Involved, as in a relationship?" She made her voice as light and carefree as possible. "No, not at all. I already told you that. Why do you ask?"

"It seemed as if you might be."

She laughed as though she found his statement humorous. Fortunately, this sounded far more genuine than her previous denial. "No, Josh, I'm not involved, I promise you, but the fact that you asked has definitely brightened my day. Okay, there was someone early on, two years ago, but we only went out for a few months and then decided to drop the whole thing."

"Really?"

"Yes, it was nothing," she assured him. "Wait until you see Red Springs," she continued excitedly. "It's small-town America, just the way I always thought it would be. Everyone's so friendly and caring."

"It seems like a nice town," he said politely.

"It is. The folks around here are good salt-of-the-earth people."

"Actually . . ." He paused again. "I, uh, thought it might be a little boring—hardly any restaurants or clubs. I mean, what do you do for entertainment? Besides, I thought you were a city girl."

"I am. . . . I was. And for entertainment, we have bingo and the county fair and—"

"If you had the opportunity, you'd move back to the city, right?" He made it more statement than question.

"Oh, sure," she responded without much consideration. Almost as soon as the words were out of her mouth, she wondered if that was entirely true. Joy loved Wyoming and everything she'd learned about life in a town like Red Springs. She'd made friends and felt she'd become part of the community.

"I phoned to let you know that my travel plans have been confirmed," Josh said. He seemed to expect her to comment.

Joy tore her gaze away from the empty pie tin. "That's good news," she said, wondering what, exactly, he wanted her to say. "I look forward to seeing you," she said, although that seemed oddly formal. Tucking the portable phone between her shoulder and her ear, she walked over to the refrigerator and opened the bottom bin, where she found a bag of Granny Smith apples. She counted out six.

"Joy?"

If Josh had asked her something, she hadn't heard it. "I'm sorry, I missed what you said."

"Perhaps I should call another time. Or I'll e-mail you."

"Fine," she said.

"Bye."

She set the apples on the counter. "Bye," she echoed, and realized Josh had hung up. He hadn't even waited until she'd said goodbye. Then again, maybe she'd kept *him* waiting a little too long.

Chapter Nine

"Are you going into town?" Tom asked Lonny late Friday afternoon as they rode toward the barn.

"I guess so," Lonny said. He'd been in the saddle from dawn, they both had, and he wasn't in any mood to shower and drive all the way into Red Springs. Something cold to drink and a hot soak would suit him just fine. Still, Letty would have his hide if he didn't show up for that auction. The entire town would be there. The bake sale auction had been hyped on the radio all week by Honey Sue Jameson, and Chase told him the original idea had been Letty's. Nope, he wouldn't dare disappoint her, or he'd have Chase mad at him, too. Not to mention that it was his one chance to make things right with Joy.

"If you do, could I tag along?" Tom asked.

This surprised Lonny, since Tom didn't often ask for favors. Little by little, he'd revealed some of what his home life had been like. Lonny knew it was a sign of trust that the boy had confided in him at all. Based on what Tom had said, he was much better off not living with his father. Lonny wanted to help him in whatever way he could. Tom was smart and should be in college or trade school. He'd brought that up a couple of times. The best person to talk to was a high school counselor—or maybe Joy. She related well to kids and knew a lot more than he did about scholarships and educational opportunities.

Tom had a real knack for horsemanship and an intuitive connection with animals. His patience and skill impressed Lonny; without much difficulty he could see Tom as a veterinarian. He'd mentioned it one evening and Tom had gotten flustered and quickly changed the subject. Later Tom had said it was best not to get his hopes up about anything like that. He had no chance of ever going to school, no matter how long he worked or how much money he saved. But Lonny felt there had to be a solution, and he was determined to find it.

"You can come along if you want," Lonny told him. He didn't ask for an explanation but suspected Tom's interest had to do with Michelle Larson. Which reminded him—he'd promised Charley Larson he'd speak to the boy about that dance.

"Thanks," Tom mumbled as he headed off to his room in the barn.

"Be ready in an hour," Lonny shouted after him.

Tom half turned, nodding.

Lonny finished tending to Moonshine, his gelding, and then hurried into the house for a long, hot shower. The mirror was fogged when he got out and began to shave. Normally he took care of that in the morning, but tonight he wanted his skin to be smooth in case—his thoughts came to a shuddering halt. In case he had the opportunity to kiss Joy again. It wasn't likely to happen, but he couldn't help hoping. He frowned. He'd rather tangle with a porcupine, he told himself, than cross her again.

Lonny snickered out loud. That wasn't true and it was time he fessed up. Not once had he stopped thinking about Joy. She was on his mind every minute of every day. It was her face, her eyes, that he saw when he drifted off to sleep at night, and her rose-scented perfume he thought about. When he woke in the morning, the first thing that popped into his mind was the memory of holding her and the kisses they'd shared. She was there all the times in between, too. Lonny didn't like it. Not thinking about her was a losing battle, so he figured he'd give in and try to win her over. As he'd told Letty, he'd blown it with Joy. Lonny Ellison wasn't a quitter, though. He hadn't gotten all those rodeo buckles by walking away from a challenge, and he wasn't about to start now. Not that he'd compare Joy Fuller to an ornery bull or an angry bronc. Well, not really. He chuckled at the thought.

By the time he'd shaved—fortunately without nicking himself—changed into a clean pair of Levi's and a stiff new shirt Letty had bought him last Christmas, Lonny figured he was well on his way to showing off his better side. No matter what Joy said or did, Lonny was determined not to lose his temper.

Tom was outside, leaning against the pickup, when

Lonny stepped out of the house and bounded down the back steps. The boy had dressed in his best clothes, too. As soon as Lonny appeared, Tom hopped into the passenger seat.

"You goin' to the bake auction?" Lonny asked conversationally.

Tom had the window rolled down, his elbow resting on the narrow ledge. "I was thinking about it," he admitted.

"Me, too. I got a hankering for something sweet."

Tom didn't comment.

"Nothing like home-baked goods."

Tom offered him a half smile and nodded in agreement.

"Will Michelle Larson be there?" Lonny asked. That question got an immediate rise out of Tom. He jerked his elbow back inside the truck and straightened abruptly.

"Maybe," he answered, glaring at Lonny as if he resented the question. "What about Miss Fuller?"

That caught Lonny unawares. Apparently Tom knew more about him than he'd assumed. "I suppose she might be," he grumbled in reply. His hired hand's message had been received, and Lonny didn't ask any further questions.

In fact, neither of them said another word until they reached town. Lonny suspected there'd be a good audience for the charity event, but he hadn't expected there'd be so much traffic around the community center that he'd have trouble getting a parking spot. As soon as they found a vacant space—ten minutes later—and parked, Tom climbed out of the truck. With a quick wave, he disappeared into the crowd.

Lonny didn't know how Tom intended to get home, but if his hired hand wasn't worried about it, then he wasn't, either.

When Lonny entered the community center, it was hard to tell there was a bingo game in progress. People roamed about the room, chatting and visiting, while Bill Franklin struggled to be heard over the chatter. A table, loaded with a delectable display of homemade goodies, was set up on stage.

Bill did his best to call out the bingo numbers but ended up having to shout into the microphone. This was possibly the biggest turnout for a bingo event in Red Springs history.

Goldie Frank stood up and shouted, "Bingo!" then proceeded to wave her card wildly.

Bill seemed downright relieved. There was a chorus of groans as Goldie came forward to accept her prize.

"That's the end of the first round of bingo for the evening," Bill said loudly, the sound system reverberating as he did. "There will now be a baked goods auction to raise funds for the carnival. Don Jameson from 1050 AM radio is our auctioneer."

That announcement was followed by a polite round of applause. Don Jameson stepped up to the front of the room and Bill handed him the microphone.

Lonny saw Letty and Chase and noticed there was an empty chair at their table. Weaving his way through the crowd, he took the opportunity to search for Joy, trying not to be too obvious. He half hoped she'd be sitting with his sister. She wasn't. When he did find her, she was with Carol Anderson. The two women sat near the back, and Joy seemed to be enjoying herself, chatting animatedly with Carol and her husband.

Lonny nearly stumbled over his own feet. It'd been nearly a week since he'd seen Joy. For the life of him, he couldn't remember her being that pretty. It occurred to him then that he'd always found her attractive, but never more than now. He took a second look. Hot damn! His sister was easy on the eyes and so were a few other women in town; Joy, however, was striking. In fact, she was beautiful.

"Lonny?" Someone tugged at his sleeve.

Letty's voice broke into his thoughts, and he realized he'd stopped dead in the middle of the room, staring at Joy Fuller with his mouth practically hanging open.

"Chase and I saved you a seat."

Despite Letty's insistent tone, he couldn't drag his eyes from Joy. Unfortunately she happened to glance up just then. The room's noise faded away as they stared at each other.

A few seconds later, Joy narrowed her eyes and deliberately turned away. It was as if she was shutting him out, closing herself off. He blinked and finally dropped his gaze.

"Lonny," his sister said again, tugging at his arm. "Did you hear me?"

"I'm coming," he muttered. He didn't need to look

back at Joy to know she was watching him. He could sense that she didn't want him there.

Her attitude didn't bode well for any conciliatory effort on his part. Still, he was up to the challenge, no matter how difficult she made it.

After exchanging greetings with Chase, Lonny took the chair next to Letty and focused his attention on the table of baked goods. As he studied the display, it occurred to him that he might not know what Joy had baked.

"Those peanut butter cookies look appetizing, don't they?" his sister whispered, leaning toward him.

"I suppose." Plenty of the other goodies did, as well.

"The apple pie, too."

There appeared to be several apple pies.

"The pie closest to the front is the one you should notice."

"Oh." It took Lonny far longer than it should have to understand what his sister was trying to tell him. He brightened. "Peanut butter, you say." Now that he thought about it, he recalled a conversation about peanut butter cookies. . . .

Letty winked and he smiled back conspiratorially.

Generally speaking, a cookie was a cookie, as far as Lonny was concerned. Right then and there, however, he had the worst hankering for peanut butter. Of course, they could've been made with sawdust and Lonny wouldn't have cared.

The first item up for auction was Betty Sanders's butterhorn rolls. Chase made the first bid of twenty dollars for the entire batch. Another hand went up, and there were three or four other bids in quick succession. In the end Chase got the rolls but it cost him nearly fifty bucks.

He stood and withdrew his wallet, grumbling all the while that he preferred it when he could meet Betty in the parking lot and buy what he wanted before anyone else had a chance.

The next item up was a coconut cake baked by Mary and Michelle Larson. It didn't come as any surprise when Tom made the opening bid. Two or three others entered the bidding, but just when it seemed that Tom was about to walk away with the cake, someone else doubled the bid. Lonny whirled around and saw that it was Al Brighton's boy, Kenny, who'd stepped in at the last minute. Kenny got to his feet, glaring across the room at Tom, who stood at the back of the hall. Tom shrugged and bid again. The room watched as the two teenage boys squared off. When the bid reached a hundred dollars, Mary Larson hurried up to the stage and whispered in Don Jameson's ear.

"Mary has offered to bake a second coconut cake," Don announced, "so you can each have one. Is that agreeable?"

Kenny's body language said it wasn't. He looked at Tom, and Tom nodded.

"All right," Kenny conceded with bad grace.

Don's gavel hit the podium as he said into the microphone, "Two coconut cakes for one hundred dollars each."

The room erupted into chaotic noise.

"This is getting a little rich for my blood," Letty whispered to Lonny.

As luck would have it, Joy's peanut butter cookies came on the auction block next. Don hadn't even begun to describe them when Lonny's hand shot into the air. "Fifty dollars," he called out.

The room went quiet.

After the two previous bids, no one seemed interested in raising the amount and that suited him just fine. Lonny sighed with relief.

"Fifty-one," a female voice said.

Frowning, Lonny craned his neck to see who was bidding against him. To his utter astonishment, it was Joy Fuller.

"Sixty," he shouted, annoyed that she'd do this.

"Sixty-one," was her immediate response.

Don glanced from one to the other. "Just a minute, Miss Fuller, aren't you the one who donated these cookies?"

"I am," she told him. "Now I want them back."

What she wanted was to make sure Lonny didn't buy them. "What's she doing that for?" he asked his sister.

Letty looked as puzzled as he did. "I don't have a clue."

"Seventy dollars," Lonny offered. If she wanted to bid him up, then there was nothing he could do about it, except to keep going. The money would benefit the community. His sister seemed to think this would help in his efforts to settle his dispute with Joy, so her bidding against him made no sense.

"Seventy-one," she called back.

Letty frowned and covered Lonny's hand with her own. "Let Joy have them," she whispered.

"But . . ." Lonny hated to lose, and it went against the grain to let her have those cookies. Surely Joy could see what he was trying to do here! Lonny didn't understand her actions; still, he figured he should trust Letty. He backed down so Joy could have the winning bid on her own peanut butter cookies.

He saw her come forward and collect the cookies. Then she immediately made her way to the exit and slipped outside.

"I'll be right back," he whispered to Letty as he quickly got up and followed.

It took him a few minutes to find her in the community center parking lot, which was dark and quiet. Lonny could hear the auction taking place inside, could hear Don's amplified voice and the din of laugher and bursts of applause. By the time he reached her, Joy had unlocked her car.

"Joy, wait," Lonny called. Then, thinking he should tread lightly, he amended his greeting. "Miss Fuller." He felt as if he were back in grade school and didn't like it.

She tensed, standing outside her little green PT Cruiser. Her purse and the tin of cookies were inside, resting on the passenger seat.

"What do you want *now?*" she demanded, crossing her arms.

She was already mad at him, and he hadn't done a damned thing wrong. "Why'd you do that?" he asked, genuinely curious. "Why'd you bid against me?"

She didn't answer him; instead she asked a question of her own. "Why can't you just leave me alone?"

"I don't know," he said with a shrug. "I guess I've gotten used to having you around."

She cracked a smile. "I couldn't let you buy those cookies."

"Why not?" Lonny didn't get this at all. Frowning, he shoved his hands inside his jeans pockets. "Do you dislike me that much?"

Her eyes shot up to meet his and she slowly shook her head. "No." Her voice was barely audible. "I don't dislike you, Lonny. I never have. It's just that—"

"Is it because I called you skinny?"

She assured him that wasn't the reason. "It isn't because of the accident, either," she said.

"Do you mind giving me a clue, then?"

For a moment he feared she was going to ignore his question. "I forgot the salt," she finally told him.

"Excuse me?"

"The salt," she said, more loudly this time. "Just before the auction today, I took out a cookie to sample. I hadn't tasted one earlier and when I did, I realized what I'd done. It was too late to withdraw them or to bake a new batch." She sighed despondently. "I was working so hard to impress you and then to do something stupid like that . . ."

She wanted to impress him? This was exactly the

kind of news he'd been hoping to hear. He propped one foot against her car bumper. "Really?"

Her gaze narrowed. "Get that smug look off your face," she snapped.

Now he knew why she'd given him the evil eye earlier. That had been a warning not to bid on her cookies, only he hadn't been smart enough to figure it out. Actually he was glad he'd bid.

Her eyes glistened as if she were about to cry. Lonny had dealt with his share of difficult situations over the years. He'd delivered calves in the middle of a lightning storm, dealt with rattlesnakes, faced drunken cowboys—but he couldn't handle a weeping woman.

"I would've eaten every one of those cookies and not said a word," he told Joy. Then, wanting to comfort her, he gently drew her into his arms.

Joy stared wordlessly up at him for a moment. She started to say something, then stopped. Frankly he'd rather she didn't speak because he could tell from the look in her eyes that she wanted the same thing he did. He brought his mouth to hers.

He heard her moan or maybe that was him. This— holding her in his arms, kissing her—was what he'd been thinking about all week, what he'd been dreaming about, too.

Her mouth was soft and pliable and responsive. She raised her arms and circled his neck, and that was all the encouragement Lonny needed. Immediately he deepened the kiss, locking his arms around her waist.

She moaned again, quietly at first, and then a bit

louder. Lonny pulled her tight against him so she'd know exactly what she was doing to him and how much he wanted her.

Suddenly, without the slightest hint, she broke off the kiss and took two paces back. At first Lonny was too stunned to react. He stared at her, hardly knowing what to think.

She was frowning. "That shouldn't have happened," she muttered.

"Why not?" He found her reaction incomprehensible because his was completely the opposite. As far as he was concerned, this was the best thing that had happened to him in two years.

"We—we don't get along."

"It seems to me we're getting along just great. Okay, so we had a rocky start, but we're over that. I'm willing to give it another shot if you are."

"I . . . I—"

She seemed to be having a problem making up her mind. That got him thinking she could use a little help, so he kissed her again.

When the kiss ended, he gave her a questioning look; wide-eyed, she blinked up at him.

Just to be on the safe side, he brought her into his embrace a third time. Once he'd finished, she was trembling in his arms.

"Let me know when you decide," he whispered, then turned and walked away.

Pleased with himself, Lonny strolled toward his pickup. As he neared the Ford, he saw his ranch hand leaning against the fender, head lowered.

"You ready to go?" Lonny asked.

Tom nodded, climbing into the truck. Only when the interior light went on did Lonny notice that he had a bloody nose. A bruise had formed on his cheek, too.

"You been fighting?" he asked, shocked by the boy's appearance.

Tom didn't answer.

"What happened?"

Tom remained silent.

"You don't want to talk about it?"

Tom shrugged.

"My guess is this involves a woman," Lonny said, starting the engine. His guess went further than that—Michelle and Kenny Brighton were part of the story. Was Michelle having trouble choosing between Tom and Kenny? It struck him as highly possible. Because he knew from the events of this evening that women seldom seemed to know what they wanted.

Chapter Ten

Joy couldn't believe she'd let Lonny Ellison kiss her again—and again. She didn't understand why she hadn't stopped him. It was as if her brain had gone to sleep or something and her body had taken over. As she lay in bed on Saturday morning after a restless night's sleep, she was aghast at her own behavior. Groaning, with the blankets pulled all the way up to her chin, she relived the scene outside the community center.

She could only imagine what Lonny must be thinking. She hadn't even been able to answer a simple question! He'd as much as said he was willing to start their relationship over and asked if she wanted that, too. She should've said she didn't want anything to do with him, although her heart and, yes, her hormones were telling her *yes*.

As soon as they were kissing—okay, be honest, *heatedly* kissing—she'd panicked. First, she and Lonny Ellison had nothing in common, and secondly . . . well, secondly— She put a halt to her reasoning because the truth was, she had no logical explanation for her response to his kisses. It wasn't like this two years ago. Okay, their kisses back then had been pleasant but not extraordinary. Not at all.

Maybe she'd gone without tenderness or physical affection for too long. That, however, wasn't true. She'd received no shortage of invitations and had dated various men in the past year. There'd been Earl Gross and Larry Caven and George Lewis. She'd dated all three for short periods of time. She'd kissed each of them, too. Unfortunately, there hadn't been any spark and the three men seemed to recognize it just as Joy had. She remained friendly with all of them, and they with her. Two years ago, there hadn't been what she'd call sparks with Lonny Ellison, either. Unless that referred to their arguments. . . .

Now Lonny was back in her life and this couldn't have come at a worse time. Not only would Josh be vis iting, he seemed interested in resuming their relationship. Once he was in town and they'd had a chance to talk, she'd know if there was a chance for them. Until then, she'd have to deal with her ambivalent feelings for Lonny.

Tossing aside her covers, she prepared a pot of coffee and while she waited, she logged on to her computer. She checked her e-mail, scrolling down the entries, and paused when she came to a message from Josh. Another entry caught her attention, too, one from Letty. She read Letty's first.

From: Letty Brown
Sent: Saturday, May 27, 2006 6:45 a.m.
To: Joy Fuller
Cc:
Subject: Where Did You Go?
Joy:
I looked for you last night after the auction and couldn't find you. My brother disappeared about the same time you did.

Joy groaned and wondered if anyone else had noticed that they'd both left just after the bidding on her peanut butter cookies.

In case you're wondering, the auction was a big hit. Your apple pie sold for $30.00 to Clem Russell, but the highest price paid for any one item was Myrtle Jameson's chocolate cake, which went for a whopping $175.00. (Unless you count the Larsons' coconut cake, which sold twice, to Tom and Kenny Brighton.) All in all, we raised more than a thousand dollars, which makes this the most successful fund-raising event ever. I wish you'd been there to the end.

Is everything all right? My brother didn't cause any problems, did he? Oh, did you hear about the fight? Tom, Lonny's ranch hand, got beaten up—three against one. Apparently Kenny and a couple of other boys were involved. I think it might've had something to do with Michelle Larson. Did you see or hear anything? That happened around the time you left. Bill Franklin broke it up and told Chase about it later.

I'll be in town later this morning. If I have time, I'll drop by. Chase and Lonny will be gone most of the day, since they're moving the cattle, trying to get the herd to the best pastureland.

Hope to catch up with you later.

Letty

Joy quickly answered her friend and told Letty she'd be in and out of the house all day, so if she did stop by Joy couldn't guarantee she'd be home. In her response, Joy ignored the subject of the auction and why she'd left.

Joy said she didn't know about the teenagers fighting; she didn't add that she'd heard something as she hurried to the parking lot. That was just before Lonny caught up with her. Needless to say, she didn't mention that, either. The less said about Friday night, the better.

As she hit the Send key, Joy realized she was avoiding her friend because of Lonny. That was a mistake. Letty had become her best friend in Red Springs, and Joy was determined not to let Letty's brother come between them.

At least Letty's e-mail assured her that Lonny would be on the range all day. Knowing there was no possibility of running into him, she was free to do her errands without worrying about seeing him every time she turned a corner.

Her first order of business was stocking up on groceries. Last week, in her effort to escape Lonny, she'd purchased the bare essentials and fled. Now she was out of milk, bread, peanut butter and almost everything else.

After downing a cup of coffee, Joy dressed in jeans and a light blue cotton shirt. At a little after nine, she headed out the door, more carefree than she'd felt in weeks. As usual, she saw a number of her students and former students on Main Street and in the grocery store. She enjoyed these brief interactions, which reminded her how different her life was compared to what it would've been if she'd stayed in Seattle.

Not until she'd loaded her groceries did she remember that she hadn't even read or responded to Josh's e-mail. It was only natural to blame that on Lonny, too. Preoccupied with him as she was, she'd forgotten all about Josh.

The first thing she'd do once she got home was log

back on to the Internet. Not responding was rude, and she was annoyed with herself for being so thoughtless.

One thing was certain—this kissing had to stop. Enough was enough. Both times they'd been standing in a parking lot, exposed to the entire community.

Oh, no.

The potential for embarrassment overwhelmed her as she slammed the trunk lid of her PT Cruiser. There'd been a fight near the community center—which meant people had been outside, maybe more than a few. So it was possible that . . . oh, dear . . . that someone had seen her and Lonny wrapped in each other's arms. At the time it had seemed so . . . so private. There they were, the two of them, in this . . . this passionate embrace, practically devouring each other. Her face burned with mortification.

No—she was overreacting. People kissed in public all the time. Red Springs was a conservative town, but she hadn't done anything worthy of censure. The only logical course of action was to put the matter out of her mind. If, by chance, she and Lonny had been seen, no one was likely to ask her about it.

"Hello, Miss Fuller." Little Cassie Morton greeted her as she skipped past Joy.

Cassie had been her student the year before and Alicia, her mother, was a classroom volunteer. Joy liked Alicia and appreciated the many hours she'd helped in class.

"Hi," Joy said cheerfully. "I see you two are out and about early on this lovely Saturday morning."

"We're going grocery shopping," Cassie explained, hopping from one foot to the other. The nine-year-old never stood still if she could run, jump or skip.

Smiling, Alicia strolled toward Joy. "Looks like you and Lonny Ellison are an item these days," the other woman said casually as she reached inside her purse and withdrew a sheaf of store coupons.

"Who told you that?" Joy asked, hoping to sound indifferent and perhaps slightly amused.

Alicia glanced up. "You mean you aren't?"

"I . . . I used to date Lonny. We went out a couple of years ago, but that's it." Joy nearly stuttered in her rush to broadcast her denial.

"Really?" Alicia's face took on a confused expression. "Sorry. I guess I misunderstood."

Joy hurried after her. "Who said we were seeing each other, if you don't mind my asking?"

"No one," Alicia told her. "I saw Lonny watching you at the auction last night and he had the *look,* if you know what I mean. It was rather sweet."

"Lonny?" Joy repeated with forced joviality. "I'm sure he was staring at someone else."

Alicia shrugged. "Maybe. You could do worse, you know. Folks around here are fond of Lonny. People still talk about his rodeo days. The Wyoming Kid was one of the best bull-riders around before he retired. I think he was smart to get out while he could still walk." She flashed a quick grin. "Actually, he was at the top of his form. That takes courage, you know, to give up that kind of money and fame. His dad wasn't doing well, and he was needed at home. Lonny returned, and he hasn't left since. I admire him for that."

"I do, too," Joy said, and it was true. She'd heard plenty about Lonny's successes, riding broncs as well as bulls. In fact, when they first dated, he'd proudly shown her his belt buckles. He wasn't shy about letting her know exactly how good he'd been. And yet, he'd abandoned it all in order to help his family. Walked away from the fame and the glory without question when his parents needed him. But he'd never mentioned that to her, not once.

"Lonny's a real sweetheart," Alicia said warmly.

Joy just nodded, unable to come up with an appropriate response, and returned to her car. Her next stop was the cleaners, where she picked up her pink pantsuit, the one she planned to wear the day Josh arrived. From there, she went to Wal-Mart for household odds and ends. By the time she'd finished, it was after twelve, and Joy was famished.

Eating a container of yogurt in front of her computer, she logged back on to the Internet and answered Josh. He'd be in Red Springs in six days. There was a lot riding on this visit—certainly for her, and maybe for him, too.

The rest of her day was uneventful. In between weekly tasks like mopping the kitchen floor and dealing with accumulated clutter, she did three loads of wash, mowed her lawn and washed her car. By dinnertime, she was pleasantly tired. She wouldn't have any problem sleeping tonight; she'd made sure of it.

The phone rang only once, late in the afternoon. It was Patsy Miller, president of the PTA. Patsy asked Joy if she'd be willing to serve as a chaperone for the high school's end-of-the-year dance.

"I'll have company," she explained reluctantly, hating to turn Patsy down. Patsy had provided consistent support to every teacher in town, and Joy wanted to repay that.

"Bring your guest," Patsy suggested.

"You wouldn't mind?"

"Not at all."

"That would be great. I'll ask him and let you know." As soon as Joy hung up, she went back on-line and told Josh about the dance. It would be the perfect end to a perfect day, or so she hoped. Joy couldn't think of any better way to show him the town she'd grown to love than to have him accompany her to the carnival and then the dance.

Climbing into bed, Joy went instantly to sleep—the contented sleep of a hardworking woman.

The next morning, she discovered that Josh had answered her two e-mails. Both the carnival and the dance sounded like fun to him, he said. He emphasized how eager he was to see her again—a mutual feeling, she thought with a smile.

When Joy arrived at church on Sunday morning, her spirits were high. Sitting in the front pew for easy access to the organ, Joy couldn't see who was and wasn't in attendance. Normally she wouldn't care. But her weekend so far had been relatively stress-free, and she wanted to keep it that way. If Lonny Ellison was at church, she needed to know for her own self-protection.

When the opening hymns were over, Joy slid off the organ bench and took the opportunity to scan the congregation. Letty and Chase sat in a middle pew; Cricket would be at the children's service in the church basement.

Without being obvious—at least she hoped not—Joy took one more look around the congregation. As far as she could tell, there was no Lonny. It seemed to her that he usually attended, so perhaps he'd decided to stay away for a week to give them both some much-needed breathing space. Her sense of well-being increased.

At the end of the announcements and just before the sermon, the choir, all dressed in their white robes, gathered at the front of the church. Joy returned to the organ bench and poised her hands over the keyboard, her eyes focused on Penny Logan, the choir director. With a nod of her head, Penny indicated that Joy should begin.

Just as she lowered her hands, she glanced over her shoulder at the church doors. At that very instant, they opened and in stepped Lonny Ellison. He stood at the back, staring directly at her. Naturally there weren't any seats available except in front; everyone knew you had to come early if you wanted to sit in the back. After a slight hesitation, Lonny started up the left-hand side—the side where Joy sat. She watched him and nearly faltered. It took all her control to play the first chord.

He'd *planned* this, darn him. Joy didn't know how

he'd managed it, but he'd timed his entrance to coincide with the music. He'd done it to unnerve her and he'd succeeded. Anger spread through her like flames in dry grass.

When she turned the sheet music, she inadvertently turned two pages instead of one. Her mistake was immediately obvious. Penny threw her a shocked look and to her credit, Joy recovered quickly. She hoped Penny was the only person who'd noticed her mistake. Still, Joy cringed in embarrassment and her heart pounded loudly. Thud. Thud. Thud. It seemed, to her ears, like a percussive counterpoint to the chords she was playing.

The rest of the service remained a blur in Joy's mind. She didn't hear a single word of Pastor Downey's sermon. Not a single word.

Thankfully, the closing song was "What a Friend We Have in Jesus," which she could've played in her sleep. As the congregation filed out, Joy finished the last refrain. She took several minutes to turn off the organ and cover the keyboard, then collect her sheet music and Bible. Normally she finished two or three minutes after the church emptied; however, this Sunday, she was at least six minutes longer than usual.

By now, she hoped, Lonny Ellison would be gone.

He wasn't.

Instead, he stood on the lawn by the church steps— waiting for her. He was chatting with a couple of other ranchers, but Joy wasn't fooled. He'd purposely hung around to talk to her.

When she walked down the steps, he broke away from his group.

Joy froze, one foot behind her on the final step, the other on the sidewalk. With a fierce look, she dared him to utter even a word. It was a glare she'd perfected in the classroom, and it obviously worked as well on adult men as it did on recalcitrant little boys. Lonny stopped dead in his tracks.

Then, as if she hadn't a care in the world, Joy casually greeted her friends and left.

Chapter Eleven

Sunday morning before he drove to church, Lonny had come into the barn to ask Tom if he wanted to attend services with him. Tom had gone a couple of Sundays, mainly because he'd hoped to see Michelle. The bruise on his cheek had turned an ugly purple and was even more noticeable now. Still, it looked worse than it felt. Kenny had sucker punched him with the aid of two of his friends, who'd distracted Tom.

Tom had declined Lonny's invitation. He didn't want Michelle to see the bruise, didn't want her to think Kenny was tougher than he was.

Tom hated fights, but he wouldn't back down from one, either. Kenny had started it, and while Tom might be small and wiry, he knew how to defend himself. He guessed Kenny Brighton had gotten the shock of his life when Tom's first punch connected. In fact, he would've smiled at the thought—except that it hurt to smile. If Bill Franklin hadn't broken up the fight, Tom would've won, despite the assistance provided by Kenny's friends. His drunk of an old man had taught him a thing or two in that department; by the time he was fifteen, Tom had learned to hold his own. Even three to one, he figured he'd stand a chance.

Lonny drove off, and Tom busied himself sweeping the barn floor. Ten mintues later, he heard another car coming down the drive and glanced out. When he saw who it was, he sucked in his breath.

Michelle.

He hesitated, then reluctantly stepped into the yard. He stood there stiffly, hands tucked in his back pockets.

She parked the car and when she got out, he realized that she'd brought him the coconut cake, protected by a plastic dome like the kind they had in diners. Catching sight of him, she frowned. Her pretty blue eycs went soft with concern as she looked at the bruise on his cheek. "Oh, Tom," she said, walking toward him.

She reached out to stroke his cheek, but he averted his face, jerking his chin away before she could touch him. At his rejection, pain flashed in her eyes. "I—I brought the cake you bought at the bake sale."

"Thanks." He took it carefully from her hands.

He figured she'd leave then, but she didn't.

"I'll put it in the house," he mumbled.

"Okay."

Tom hurried into the kitchen, depositing the cake on the table. She and her mother had done a good job with it, making it almost double the size of the one Kenny had claimed Friday night. That pleased Tom.

"What are you still doing here?" he asked gruffly when he returned to the yard. He didn't want her to know how happy he was to see her—despite his injury and his disfigured face.

"I came to find out if Kenny hurt you."

She should worry about the other guy, not him, he thought defiantly. "He didn't."

Her eyes refused to leave his face and after a moment, she nearly dissolved into tears. "I'm so sorry, Tom."

"For what? You weren't to blame."

"Yes, I was," she cried, and her voice quavered. "It was all my fault."

Tom shook his head, angry that she'd assume responsibility. Kenny Brighton was the jerk, not Michelle.

"Kenny asked me to the dance and I told him no. He wanted to know why I wouldn't go with him and I . . . I said I . . . I was going with you."

Tom felt his throat close up. "I already told you I can't take you to the dance." He didn't mean to sound angry, but he couldn't help it.

"I know, and I'm truly sorry, but I had to tell Kenny *something,* otherwise he'd pester me. He wouldn't leave me alone until I gave in and I . . . I know I shouldn't have lied. But because I did, he had it in for you and when you bid on the cake, he was mad and started that fight."

She was crying openly now. The tears ran down her face and Tom watched helplessly. He'd only seen one other woman cry—his mother—and he hadn't been able to stand it. He'd always tried to protect her, to comfort her. So Tom did what came naturally, and that was to hold Michelle.

They'd never touched. All their relationship amounted to was a few conversations at the feed store. He'd liked other girls back home, but he'd never had strong feelings for any of them the way he did Michelle.

When she slipped so easily into his arms, it was all Tom could do to hold in a sigh. She wrapped her arms about his waist and pressed her face against his shirt. Tom shyly put his own arms around her and rested his jaw against her hair. She smelled fresh and sweet and he'd never felt this good.

Michelle sniffled, then dropped her arms. He did the same. "I should go," she whispered.

Tom didn't say anything to stop her, but he didn't want her to leave.

She started walking toward her car. "I didn't tell my parents where I was going and . . ." She kept her head lowered and after a short pause blurted out, "Why won't you go to the dance with me?"

Dread sat heavily on his chest. "I . . . can't."

"You don't like me?"

He laughed, not because what she asked had amused him, but because it was so ludicrous, so far removed from the truth. "Oh, I like you."

She gazed up at him and he swore her eyes were the pure blue of an ocean he'd never seen, and deep enough to dive straight into. "I like you, too," she told him in a whisper. "I like you a *lot*. I wait for you every week, just hoping you'll stop by with Lonny. Dad thinks I'm working all these extra hours because I'm saving money for college. That's not the real reason, though. I'm there on the off-chance you'll come into town."

Although he was secretly thrilled, Tom couldn't allow her to care for him. He had nothing to offer her. He had no future, and his past . . . his past was something he hoped to keep buried for the rest of his life. "I'm nothing, Michelle, you hear me? Nothing."

"Don't say that," she countered with a firmness that surprised him. "Don't *ever* say that, because it's not true. I've seen you with people and with animals, too. You're respectful and caring and kind. You don't want anyone to see it, but you are. You're not afraid of work, either. Kenny comes to the store with his dad, but he lets other people load up the truck. You're the first one there, willing to help. I've noticed many things about you, Tom. *Many* things," she emphasized. "You're as honorable as my father."

That appeared to be the highest compliment she could pay him. Tom didn't say it, but he'd noticed many things about Michelle Larson, too. What he liked most was the way she believed in him. No one ever had, except his mother. By the time she died, though, she'd been beaten down and miserable. Tom had been determined to get away from the man who'd done that to her—his father—the man who'd tried to destroy him, too. There was no turning back now.

126

The pressure on his chest increased. "I'll see what I can do about that dance," he said. He couldn't make her any promises. More than anything, he wanted to go there with Michelle. More than anything he wanted an excuse to hold her again, and smell her hair and maybe even kiss her.

"Thank you," she whispered.

Then before he could stop her, she pressed the palm of her hand against his cheek. His jaw still ached a bit. Not much; just enough to remind him that Kenny Brighton was a dirty fighter and not to be trusted. Taking her wrist, Tom brought her hand to his lips and kissed it.

Michelle smiled and it seemed—it really did—as if the sun had come out from behind a dark cloud and drenched him in warmth and light. But when she left soon afterward, the sensation of buoyant happiness quickly died. He should never have told her he'd think about the dance.

An hour later, Lonny returned from church and without a word to Tom marched directly into the house. Tom didn't know what was wrong and Lonny hadn't confided in him. Lonny was fair and a good boss, but he hadn't been in a particularly good mood for the last week or so. Not that it made him rude or unpleasant. Just kind of remote.

At twelve-thirty, Tom went inside. They took turns preparing meals, and this one was his. Tom found Lonny sitting at the kitchen table, his head in his hands, almost as if he was praying.

127

"You feel okay?" Tom asked, wondering what he could do to help.

Lonny shrugged. "I guess."

Tom opened the refrigerator and took out a slab of cheese. Grilled cheese sandwiches were easy enough. That and a can of soup would take care of their appetites.

"How many sandwiches you want?" he asked.

"Just one."

Tom nodded and took bread out of the plastic container on the kitchen counter. "I heard there's going to be a dance in town," he said, hoping he sounded casual and only vaguely interested.

"You thinking of going?" Lonny asked, showing the first hint of curiosity.

Tom shrugged, imitating Lonny. "I was thinking about it. Only . . ." He didn't finish.

"Only what?"

Tom lifted his shoulders again. "All I brought with me is work clothes." That was all he had, period, but he didn't mention that part.

Lonny stood up from the table and looked Tom up and down. "How much you weigh?"

Tom told him, as well as he could remember.

"That's about right. I've got an old suit you're welcome to have if it fits you."

Tom's heart shot straight into his throat. No one had ever given him anything without expecting something in return. "I'll pay you for it—I insist. How much you want for that suit? If it fits," he qualified.

"Fine, pay if you want," Lonny agreed. "I'll take a big fat slice of that as payment," he said, gesturing toward the coconut cake.

Tom grinned, satisfied with his response. "You got it."

"Fair trade. If you need a ride into town Friday night, let me know."

Tom laid the bread, butter side down, in the heated pan. "I'd appreciate it."

"You taking Michelle Larson to that dance?" Lonny asked next.

With his back to the other man, moving the sandwiches around with a spatula, Tom smiled. "Like I said, I was thinking about it."

"You do that. She's a good girl."

"I know." He frowned then, because having something decent to wear was just the first hurdle. It didn't come easy, letting anyone know how inadequate he was when it came to a situation like this. He glanced over his shoulder and saw that Lonny was watching him. "I've never been to a dance before," he muttered.

"You'll enjoy yourself," Lonny said, reaching for a knife and a couple of plates to serve slices of the cake.

"I said, I've never been to a dance before," Tom repeated, louder this time. He turned around to properly face his employer.

Lonny frowned and looked mildly guilty about slicing into Tom's coconut cake. "There's nothing to worry about. They might have a real band, or there could be someone playing CDs—I'm not sure how it'll work this

year. The school will arrange to have a few adults there as chaperones."

It was plain that Tom would need to spell it out for him. "I don't know how to dance," he murmured, breaking eye contact. "What am I supposed to do when the music starts?"

"Ah." Lonny nodded sagely. "I see your problem."

"Do *you* know how to dance?" He wouldn't come right out and ask, but if Lonny volunteered to teach him, Tom would be willing to take lessons, as long as they didn't interfere with work.

"Me, dance?" Lonny asked in a jovial tone. "Not really. Mostly I fake it."

"Anyone can do that?" Tom wasn't sure he believed this.

"I do. I just sort of shuffle my feet and move my arms around a lot and no one's ever said anything. You like music, don't you?"

Tom did. He listened to the country-western station on the radio. "What kind of music do they play at school dances?"

The question appeared to be difficult because it took Lonny a long time to answer. "Regular music," he finally said.

Tom didn't know what regular music was. He frowned.

"I've got some old movie videos in the living room somewhere that you might want to watch. They might help you."

"What kind of videos?"

Lonny thought about that for a few minutes. "There's a couple with John Travolta and one with Kevin Bacon. Hey, that movie might interest you because it's got a farm boy in it who doesn't know how to dance, either. Kevin knows a few moves and takes him under his wing. It's a good movie, great music. Why don't you watch it?"

"Okay." Tom would do just about anything to keep from making a fool of himself in front of Michelle. He needed to learn quickly, too; the dance was only five days away.

The phone rang then, and Lonny went into the other room to answer it. While he was on the phone, Tom finished preparing the cheese sandwiches. He heated a can of tomato soup and had it dished up and on the table by the time Lonny returned.

When Lonny came back into the kitchen, he was frowning.

"Problems?" Tom asked, instantly alert.

Lonny shook his head. "I'm going to volunteer as a chaperone at that dance."

Tom's suspicions were instantly raised. "Any particular reason?"

Lonny bit into his grilled cheese sandwich and nodded. "Sounds like Kenny Brighton might be looking for trouble, especially if you turn up with Michelle."

Tom bristled. "I can take care of myself."

"I don't doubt it, but Kenny will think twice about starting something if I'm there."

Tom didn't like the idea of Lonny having to hang around the school dance because of him.

Lonny seemed to sense his reaction. "What about Michelle?" he added. "How's *she* going to feel if Kenny beats up on you again?"

Tom saw the wisdom of what Lonny was saying. "You'd do that for me?" he asked.

"I offered, didn't I?"

Tom's chest tightened, and he stared down at his plate while he struggled with the emotion that hit him out of nowhere. This rancher, whom he'd known for only a few months, was more of a parent to him than his own father had ever been.

"Let me see about that suit," Lonny said when he'd eaten his lunch. He set his dirty dishes in the sink and went upstairs; within minutes he'd returned, holding out a perfectly good brown suit.

"What do you think?" Lonny asked.

The suit was far better than Tom had expected. It didn't look as if it'd ever been worn. "What I think is I should give you that entire coconut cake."

Lonny laughed. "Go try this on, and if there's any of that cake left when you get back, consider yourself fortunate."

Tom already knew he was fortunate. He didn't need a slice of coconut cake to tell him that.

Chapter Twelve

Letty and Chase often invited Lonny, and now Tom, to join them for dinner on Sunday evenings. Tom had accepted twice, but this week he declined. Before Lonny left, Tom asked if it would be all right if he watched a few of those videos Lonny had mentioned earlier.

Lonny had no objection to that. He smiled as he pulled out of the yard in his pickup and headed for Chase and Letty's. He was glad to be able to help the boy, hoping it worked out, with the dance and Michelle and all.

Lonny drove the short distance to Chase's ranch, still feeling confused about Joy. He counted on Letty to have some insights on what he should do about his feelings for her. He knew he could be stubborn, but until recently he hadn't recognized how much his attitude had cost him. For nearly two years, he'd allowed his relationship with Joy to lie fallow. During that time he'd watched her develop friendships in the community, and he knew that everything he'd accused her of was wrong. She was no city slicker; from the first, she'd done her best to become part of the community. Lonny hadn't wanted to accept that because she'd wounded his pride. He'd wanted her to fail just to prove how right he was. It bothered him to admit that, but it was the truth. He swallowed hard and his hands tightened around the steering wheel. Because of his stubbornness, he'd done a great disservice to Joy—and to himself.

Plain and simple, Lonny was attracted to Joy—more than attracted. Their kisses over the past few days confirmed what he already knew. Another uncomfortable truth—not once in the last two years had Joy been far from his thoughts. She'd always been there, just below the surface of his consciousness. Following their traffic *incident*—as she'd correctly described it—the potency of that attraction had all but exploded in his face.

Lonny had been a fool. He could acknowledge it now: for two years he'd been in love with Joy. The near-collision had simply brought everything to the surface, and it explained his overreaction to the events of that afternoon. He grinned thinking about the way he'd stormed at her as if she'd nearly caused a fatal accident. No wonder she was wary of him.

Deep in thought, Lonny missed the turnoff to the Circle C. He must've driven here ten thousand times and not once overshot the entrance. The fact that he had today said a lot about his preoccupation with Joy.

As Lonny drove into the yard, he noticed that Chase was giving Cricket a riding lesson. The little girl slowly rode a brown spotted pony around the corral while Chase held the lead rope. Chase gave him a quick wave and continued walking the girl and her pony. Meanwhile, Letty sat in a rocking chair on the porch, watching.

Lonny crossed the yard and joined his sister, claiming the rocking chair next to hers.

Letty raised her glass of lemonade in greeting. "Tom won't be coming?" she asked.

Lonny shook his head. "Not tonight."

Letty stood and went inside the house, reappearing a minute later with a second glass of lemonade, which she handed him.

"Thanks." Lonny took a long, thirst-quenching drink, then set down the glass with a disconsolate sigh.

Letty turned to him. "What's wrong?"

His state of mind obviously showed more than Lonny had realized. Rather than blurt out what was troubling him, he shrugged. "I've been doing some thinking about Joy and me."

His sister sat down again and started rocking. "I've been telling you for at least a year that you're an idiot." Her smile cut the sharpness of her words.

"I can't disagree," he muttered, disgusted with how ineptly he'd handled every aspect of this relationship. Even after being on the rodeo circuit and dating dozens of women, he was as naive as a twelve-year-old kid about establishing—no, *salvaging*—a romance with a woman like Joy.

"Listen," he said, deciding to speak honestly with his sister. "Would you be willing to advise me? Maybe you could even help me—speak to Joy on my behalf." He wouldn't normally ask that of Letty, and requesting this kind of favor didn't come easy.

Letty hesitated; she rocked back and forth, just the way their mother used to. When she spoke he heard her regret. "Lonny, as much as I'd like to, I can't do that."

He nodded. Actually, that was what he'd expected, but it didn't hurt to ask.

"I'll be happy to offer my opinion, though."

He made a noncommittal sound. Letty had never been shy about sharing her opinions, especially when they concerned him.

"There's something you should probably know. Something important I learned just today."

He tensed. "About Joy?"

Letty sipped her lemonade. "Josh Howell contacted her."

"The college boyfriend?" Lonny's jaw tightened. Right now, this was the worst piece of news he could hear. When they'd first started dating, Joy had casually mentioned Josh a few times; Lonny had read between the lines and understood that this relationship had played an important role in Joy's past.

She'd stayed in touch with Josh and although their romance had cooled, Joy still had feelings for the other man. It was early in their own relationship, and Lonny hadn't wanted Joy to think he was the jealous type, so he'd said nothing. But the fact was, he'd been jealous and hadn't liked knowing Joy and this city boy were continuing some kind of involvement, even a diminished one and even from a distance.

"Well?" Letty pressed. "Doesn't it concern you?"

Lonny made an effort to disguise his views on the matter. "What does Josh want?"

His sister didn't seem to know. "All I heard is he's coming to visit."

"Here? In Red Springs?"

"That's what she said. Apparently he wants to revive their relationship."

"She told you that?" His jaw went even tighter.

"Not in so many words, but think about it. Why else would Josh come here? It isn't like he has some burning desire to visit a ranching community. He's coming because of Joy." She paused, tilting her head toward Lonny. "I find his timing rather suspicious, don't you?"

"How?" Lonny asked bluntly.

"Joy's teaching contract is up for renewal."

"So, you think he's hoping to lure her back to Seattle?" His voice fell as he took in the significance of the timing. Right then and there, Lonny decided he wasn't letting her go without a fight. Not physical, of course—that would be stupid and unfair; Josh wouldn't stand a chance against him, if he did say so himself. And knowing Joy, she'd be furious with Lonny and immediately side with the city guy. A physical showdown would be the worst possible move. No, this challenge was mental. Emotional. And it had more to do with convincing Joy than scaring off Josh.

"When will he be here?" he asked urgently.

Letty must've seen that determined look in his eyes, because she reached over and patted his hand reassuringly. "I'm not sure, but I believe it's sometime this week."

He nodded.

"What are you thinking?" she asked.

That should be obvious. "I've only got a few days to

talk Joy into staying here." Although he knew darn well that more than talk would be involved. . . .

Letty frowned at him. "Why do you care if she leaves or not?"

Lonny didn't appreciate the question. Nevertheless, he gave her an honest answer. He could pretend he hadn't heard—or he could tell Letty the words that burned to be spoken. "Because I love her."

"I know," Letty replied, leaning back with a satisfied sigh. "You have for a long time."

Lonny expected more of an I-told-you-so comment and was mildly surprised when Letty didn't lay into him for his foolishness or recite a litany of rules on how to persuade Joy to make her life in Red Springs, with him.

"So what are you going to do about it?" Letty asked next.

The answer to that wasn't clear yet. "I don't know."

Letty frowned again, a worried frown. "Promise me you won't say anything stupid."

"Like what?" he demanded.

She rolled her eyes. "Like you're going to charge her insurance company for the so-called damage to your truck."

"I never really intended to do that. It was a ploy, that's all."

"A ploy to infuriate and anger Joy. Because of it, you've got a lot of ground to recover now."

Lonny didn't need his sister telling him what he already knew. "I'll talk to her." But that didn't seem to be working, either, he realized sadly. He'd left her a note, and she'd thrown it away. Joy wasn't interested in talking to him, yet every time they were together, they ended up in each other's arms. Lonny wasn't complaining about *that*. The fact was, those few kisses gave him hope and encouragement. They told him that while Joy might deny it, she did have feelings for him, feelings as intense as his were for her. Feelings she wasn't ready to acknowledge.

His sister turned to stare at him as if he were a stranger. "Can I make a suggestion?" she asked.

"Sure." He'd been counting on it.

"A woman likes to know that she's wanted and needed and treasured," she told him. Lonny understood what she was saying—that this was exactly how Chase felt about her. Lonny had seen it happen. His friend had come alive the moment Letty returned to Red Springs. It was the same way Lonny felt about Joy. All he had to do now was figure out how to protect *her* pride, while keeping his own intact.

"I'll tell her," Lonny said, suspecting this might be his only route to Joy.

"Go slow," Letty murmured.

"Slow," he repeated. "But I haven't got time to hang around, not with this other guy hot on her heels."

"Yes, you do, otherwise Joy will assume that you're only interested now because Josh is about to make an appearance in her life. She's got to believe your actions are motivated by sincerity, not competitiveness."

"Oh." Letty was right about that, too.

This was getting complicated. "Should I approach her with gifts?" He felt at a distinct disadvantage. Joy wasn't like the girls he'd met in his rodeo days; he'd rarely ever given them gifts, beyond maybe buying them a beer.

Letty nodded approvingly. "That's a good place to start."

Lonny rather liked the idea of bringing Joy things. He had a freezer full of meat, some of his best. None of that hormone-laden stuff sold in the grocery stores, either. He'd explain that his and Chase's cattle were lean, and fed on grass, and he'd make sure she recognized the significance of that. "I could take her some steaks from my freezer," he said, pleased with himself.

"Uh . . ." Letty cocked her head to one side, as if she was trying to come up with a way to tell him that wasn't quite what she had in mind.

"What?"

"Bringing her a few steaks is a nice thought," his sister informed him. "But women tend to prefer gifts that are more . . . *personal.*"

Lonny cast a desperate look at Letty. "Help me out here."

"Flowers are always nice," she said.

Flowers from a shop were expensive and died within a few days. "What about perfume?"

"Yes, but that poses a small problem. Most women have preferences based on experience with various scents. They develop their own favorites. A particular scent smells different depending on who wears it, you know."

Lonny wasn't sure what his sister had just said, other than that he shouldn't buy perfume. Well, if there was no better alternative, he'd go with her first suggestion. "Flowers I can do."

"Start there."

"I will," he promised. "Then you'll help me figure out what I should get her next?" he said, relying on his sister's assistance. He considered her the strategist; he'd simply follow her directions.

"Don't be in too big a rush," Letty reminded him. "If you run into her by accident, be polite and respectful, and then go about your business."

Lonny saw the brilliance of his sister's words. He hoped he could restrain himself enough to do that. Every time they were together, all he could think about was how much he wanted to hold and kiss Joy. It went without saying that there was more to a relationship between a man and a woman than the physical. Mutual desire was important and necessary, but no more so than mutual respect, honesty and genuine caring. He felt all of that for Joy. Unfortunately, the easiest part to convey was his longing to hold her and kiss her.

"Other than getting Joy gifts, what else should I do?"

Letty's brow creased in thought.

"Do I have to learn to talk pretty?" Lonny asked, a bit embarrassed. Like most cowboys, he tended to be plain-spoken. Besides, it was hard enough not to trip over his tongue saying normal things to Joy, let alone anything poetic.

"She needs to know how much she means to you," Letty said.

Lonny gestured helplessly as a sick feeling settled in the pit of his stomach. "I wouldn't know how to tell her that."

"Tell me what you like about her physically," Letty said. "And I suggest you not say anything about her weight."

"Okay . . ." A picture of Joy formed in his mind, and he relaxed. "She's just the right height."

"For what?"

Lonny shifted uncomfortably in his seat. "Kissing."

"Okay . . . anything else?"

"Oh, sure." But now that he'd said it, he couldn't come up with a single thing.

"Do you like her eyes?"

He nodded. "They're blue." He said that so Letty would know he'd been paying attention. "A real pretty shade of blue."

"Good." She clearly approved. "You can tell her that."

"Sort of a Roquefort-cheese blue."

Her face fell.

"That's not a good comparison?" he muttered.

"Think flowers instead," she hinted.

"Okay." But he'd have to give it some consideration. He wasn't that knowledgeable about flowers. Especially *blue* flowers.

"If you can persuade her, you and Joy will make a wonderful couple."

"If?" he repeated, taking offense at the qualifier. His sister seemed to forget that at one time he'd ridden bulls and wild broncos. It was the sheer force of his determination, along with—of course—his innate skill, that had kept him in prize money. Joy was the biggest prize of his life and he was going to cowboy up and do whatever he had to—even if he got thrown or trampled in the process.

"What took you so long, big brother?" Letty teased. "You've been crazy about Joy for two years."

Earlier, he would've denied that, but the time for pretense was past. "Pride mostly." He thanked God for that near-accident now. That, and their subsequent confrontation, had made him see the error of his ways. No doubt Letty was happy with his decision, and Lonny's heart felt lighter and more carefree than it had in years. He felt good. Better than good, he felt *terrific.*

Lonny followed his sister's gaze as she watched Chase and Cricket with the spotted pony. He was moved to see how much Chase loved Cricket. He might not be her biological father, but in every way that mattered, Chase was Cricket's daddy.

His sister's eyes grew soft and full of love. One day, if everything went as Lonny hoped, he'd have a son or daughter of his own. It would please him beyond measure if Joy was the mother of his children. The thought quickened a desire so powerful that his chest constricted with emotion. He loved Joy. He sincerely loved her and the sun would fall from the sky before he lost her to anyone, least of all an old boyfriend.

Chapter Thirteen

The alarm rang at six o'clock Monday morning and with a groan, Joy stretched out her arm and flipped the switch to the off position. She was warm and comfortable, and a sense of happiness spread through her. In five days, Josh would be in Red Springs. With her!

He'd phoned on Sunday afternoon, and they'd talked for an hour. Toward the end of their conversation, he'd admitted that Red Springs was two hundred-plus miles out of his way; in other words, he was letting her know that he wanted to renew their relationship. That meant he'd missed her and was willing to invest time, effort and expense in seeing her again. She felt the glow of that knowledge even now. Lonny drifted into her mind and she made a determined effort to chase him away. Her willingness to accept his kisses—and kiss him back—mortified her.

In fact, it was Lonny's kisses that had prompted her to tell Letty about Josh's visit. Letty would certainly mention it to Lonny, which was exactly what she wanted. It was the coward's way out, she freely admitted that, but she was apprehensive over what might happen when Josh arrived.

She was afraid Lonny might force a confrontation, and she hoped this news would discourage him from seeking her out again. She didn't *want* to think about Lonny or worry about her reaction to him. She felt so positive about Josh and their future together, and the only person who might ruin that was Lonny.

Josh was thoughtful and generous and as different from Lonny Ellison as a man could get. Just the thought of him incited her to toss aside the warm covers and bolt upright, irritated that this disagreeable rancher kept making unwanted appearances in her life. He was irrational, bad-tempered and, well . . . It didn't matter, because she wouldn't be having anything more to do with him.

Joy got to school early and had just parked her car in the employee lot when she saw Letty Brown drive to the student drop-off area. Either Letty had business in town this morning, or Cricket had missed the bus.

The back passenger door opened and Cricket popped out, greeted Joy with an exuberant "Hi, Miss Fuller!" and then skipped over to the playground.

Letty rolled down her car window and waved at Joy.

Joy waved back. Strangely reluctant to see her friend, she trotted over to Letty's car. Thankfully no one had pulled in behind her. In the next twenty minutes the driveway would be seething with activity.

"Morning," Letty said from inside her car.

"Isn't this a beautiful day?" It could be raining buckets and it would still be an absolutely perfect day as far as Joy was concerned. As long as she could avoid seeing, hearing or thinking about one annoying man . . .

"You seem in a very good mood for a Monday morning."

"I am," Joy said, resting one hand on the window frame.

Letty laughed. "Me, too." She lowered her voice. "Can you keep a secret?"

"Of course."

Letty bit her lower lip. "Chase doesn't even know. Cricket, either." Then her eyes brightened and she placed her hand on Joy's. "I'm pregnant!"

Joy gasped. "Oh, Letty! That's incredible news!" Because of her medical condition, pregnancy could be a risk. Letty had told Joy that Chase was concerned about the strain a pregnancy would put on her heart. He didn't want to lose her.

"I won't say anything to Chase until the doctor officially confirms it," she continued, "but I know my own body. And just to be sure, I took one of those home tests, too. Chase will want to hear what the doctor says, though."

"But I thought—" Joy closed her mouth abruptly, afraid to say anything about the worries and fears that might accompany a pregnancy.

Letty must have sensed what Joy was thinking, because she added, "I went to see the heart specialist recently."

Joy remembered that visit. It was the day Lonny had come by the school to pick up Cricket.

"The doc gave me a clean bill of health," Letty exclaimed with unrestrained happiness. "The surgery was one hundred percent successful, and he couldn't see any reason I shouldn't have a second baby."

Joy knew how badly Letty wanted another child. Seeing her friend's wild joy nearly brought tears to her own eyes. "I'm so thrilled for you."

"Now, promise me, not a word to anyone," Letty warned.

"My lips are sealed." Half leaning into the front of the vehicle through the open window, Joy hugged her friend's shoulders. Straightening, she said, "I have some news, too—although it isn't as momentous as yours."

"Is this a secret or am I free to broadcast it?"

"So you're the town crier?"

"No," Letty said with a laugh, "that would be Honey Sue, but I run a close second."

Joy waited a moment for effect, then nearly burst out laughing at the expression on Letty's face. "Josh and I talked for over an hour yesterday, and I'm thinking of moving back to Seattle." She hated to leave Red Springs. But if she and Josh decided to resume their relationship in a serious way, she'd have to return to the Puget Sound area. A few Internet inquiries had assured her there were plenty of teaching positions available.

The joy faded from Letty's eyes. "You'd actually move back to Seattle for Josh?"

Joy nodded. "Of course, everything hinges on what happens this weekend. But at this point, I'd say there's plenty of reason to believe I would."

Letty made an effort to smile. "I'd hate to see you go."

"I'd hate it, too, but I can't ask Josh to give up his career and move to Wyoming when there are no job opportunities for him. I can get a teaching position nearly anywhere."

"That makes sense." Letty's words were filled with poorly concealed disappointment.

Joy took a deep breath, realizing this had to be said. "I know you always hoped that things would work out between Lonny and me. Unfortunately that's not the case."

"My brother can be stubborn, that's for sure."

"I can be, too," Joy admitted. "The two of us don't really get along. I feel bad about it, because I genuinely like Lonny. I always have, but it's best to bow out now before either of us gets hurt."

"You're certain about that?" Letty's gaze pleaded with hers.

"Yes," Joy said quickly. Although she was confident and hopeful about her relationship with Josh, she wouldn't leave Red Springs without a few regrets. And one of those regrets was Lonny Ellison. . . .

"When will Josh arrive?" Letty asked.

Joy braced her hands against the window frame. "Friday. He's driving from Salt Lake City and should get here sometime in the afternoon."

"That's . . . great."

Joy could tell that Letty was trying hard to sound pleased for her; at the same time, the concern in her eyes sent a conflicting message.

"So Josh will be with you at the school carnival?" she asked casually.

"He's looking forward to it, and so am I."

When Letty didn't respond, Joy asked, "Do you think that'll be a problem?" Although she'd lived in the community for two years, there seemed to be a lot she didn't understand about people's expectations. Perhaps bringing a male friend to what was technically a school function would be frowned upon.

Letty gave her a slight smile. "No, everything's fine. Don't worry."

Joy smiled back but once again felt tears gather in her eyes.

"I'll miss you," Letty whispered.

"There's a chance I might not be going," Joy said honestly. "The school board's offered me a new contract and I've asked for time to think it over. I'll know more after this weekend. Oh, I shouldn't have said anything," she muttered fretfully. "It's too soon."

Letty shrugged and then sighed. "We'll keep in touch no matter what happens."

"Absolutely," Joy concurred. "We'll always be friends."

Letty nodded and glanced over her shoulder. Another car had pulled into the school's circular driveway. "You're right, of course. Anyway, I should go."

"See you later," Joy said, stepping back from the curb.

Letty checked her rearview mirror and drove carefully out of the slot.

Joy went on to her class, excited and happy for her friend. Despite his worries, Chase would be ecstatic when Letty told him about her pregnancy. Joy had watched Chase with Cricket and marveled at how deeply he cared for the child. Lonny was a good uncle, too. In time, when he found the right woman, Lonny would make a good father himself. But she didn't want to think about Lonny with another woman and pushed that thought from her mind.

Her day went relatively smoothly, considering that this was the last week of school and the children were restless and eager to be outside. When classes were dismissed that afternoon, Joy drove down Main Street to Franklin Rental. She needed to double-check that the cotton candy machine would be there in time for the carnival.

"Good afternoon, Joy," Bill Franklin greeted her when she entered the store.

She stepped around air compressors, spray paint equipment and a dozen other machines of uncertain purpose on her way to the counter. "Hello, Bill."

"I bet I know why you're here. Rest assured that I'll have everything well before Friday. If not, I'm afraid I'd be ridden out of town on a rail," he said with a laugh.

"Thanks, Bill." She smiled at his mild joke. "I'll tell the other committee members."

"Thanks, Joy."

After another few minutes, she retraced her steps

through the maze of equipment that littered the floor.

She was headed toward her parked car when she saw Lonny Ellison strolling in the direction of Franklin Rentals. She stopped cold in her tracks.

He saw her, too, and froze.

Neither moved for at least a minute.

Lonny broke out of the trance first and walked, slowly and deliberately, toward her.

Joy's heart felt as if it were attempting to break free of her chest, it pounded that hard and fast. Despite her reaction, she pretended to be unaffected—or tried to. As Lonny neared, she lowered her head and said in a stiff, formal tone, "Mr. Ellison."

Lonny paused, touching the brim of his Stetson. "Miss Fuller," he returned just as formally. Then he removed his hat and held it in both hands.

Lonny had stopped a few feet away. Joy stood there, rooted to the sidewalk. She couldn't summon the resolve to take a single step, although her nerves were on full alert and adrenaline coursed through her bloodstream.

"You look . . . pretty . . . today," Lonny said after an awkward moment.

Not once had Lonny ever complimented her appearance. "Thank you. You do, too."

His eyes widened. "I look . . . pretty?"

She almost managed a smile. "Not exactly."

"That's a relief."

This was ridiculous, she told herself, the two of them standing in the middle of the sidewalk like this, just staring at each other. "Have a good afternoon," she said abruptly and started to walk away.

"Joy," Lonny choked out.

"Yes?" Joy maintained a healthy distance for fear they'd find an excuse to kiss again, and in broad daylight, too.

He hesitated. "I—I hope the two of us will remain friends."

At first Joy wasn't sure how to respond. His evident sincerity took her by surprise. "I do, too," she finally said.

His eyes crinkled with a half smile and he nodded once, then cleared his throat. "Also, I wish to apologize if I offended you by my actions."

"Actions?"

He lowered his voice. "Those . . . kisses."

"Oh." Her cheeks instantly flushed with heat. He appeared to be awaiting her response, so she said, "Apology accepted."

"Thank you."

Her car wasn't far away now and when she used the remote to unlock it, Lonny rushed over and held open the driver's door for her.

Slipping inside the Cruiser, she blinked up at him. "Who are you and what have you done with Lonny Ellison?"

He chuckled. "I'm not nearly as bad as you think."

She wanted to say she doubted that, but it would've been impolite.

"I'm through with pretending, Joy," he told her. "I

cared about you two years ago, and I care about you now." He took a step back from her vehicle. "I let foolish pride stand in the way and I regret it." Having said that, he smiled, replacing his Stetson. "Have a good evening."

"Thank you, I will." Her fingers trembled as she inserted the key in the ignition. When she looked up again, Lonny was walking into Franklin Rentals.

Joy mulled over their short exchange during her drive home, still feeling uncertain and confused. There was an unreal quality about it, almost as if she'd dreamed the entire episode. This strained politeness wouldn't last; of that, she was sure. Sooner or later Lonny would return to his dictatorial ways.

She poured herself a glass of iced tea and sat at her kitchen table while she mentally reviewed her day, starting with Letty's news. This evening would be a very special one for Letty and Chase, since she'd be telling him about the baby.

Without warning, Joy felt a sharp twinge of emotion. One day that same pleasure would be hers, when she'd have the distinct pleasure of letting the man she loved know that she carried his child. A yearning, a deep and silent longing, yawned inside her. She felt the desire to be loved, to experience that kind of love. Out of nowhere, tears filled her eyes and she bit hard on her lower lip, trying to control the emotion.

Someday . . . She had to believe that someday it would be her turn.

Chapter Fourteen

Tom Meyerson eagerly anticipated Lonny's next trip into Red Springs. Fortunately, he didn't have long to wait. At breakfast on Wednesday morning, Lonny announced that he had several errands to run that afternoon.

"Would you mind if I came along?" Tom asked as nonchalantly as he could. It was a habit from the years of living with his father. If his old man knew that Tom wanted or needed something, he went out of his way to make sure Tom didn't get it. Through the years, Tom had gotten good at hiding his feelings.

He had to see Michelle and talk to her. He wouldn't *ask* Lonny to take him, to make a special trip for him, nor would he borrow the truck. But if Lonny was going anyway . . . Sure, he could phone Michelle and he probably should have, but he wanted to see her eyes light up when he told her he'd be taking her to the dance, after all. At night, as he drifted into sleep, he imagined her smile and it made him feel good inside.

He waited for Lonny to answer, almost fearing his employer would turn him down.

Lonny shrugged. "As long as you're finished your chores, I don't have a problem with you hitching a ride."

Tom smiled, unable to disguise his happiness. He cleared his throat. "Thanks, I appreciate it."

Lonny slapped him on the back in an affectionate gesture. Before he could stop himself, Tom flinched. After years of avoiding his father's brutal assaults, the reaction was instinctive. He held his breath, hoping Lonny wouldn't comment.

Lonny noticed, all right, but to Tom's relief, didn't say anything. Instead, he checked his watch. "I want to leave around four."

Michelle would be out of school by then and at the store, working in the office for her dad. Happy expectation carried Tom the rest of the day.

He'd watched the videos Lonny had mentioned two or three times each and had practiced a few moves in front of the mirror. No one was going to confuse him with Kevin Bacon or John Travolta, that was for sure. But he didn't feel like a complete incompetent, either.

He'd been listening to the radio more, too, and was beginning to think he could handle a dance. Deep down, he sensed that his mother would be pleased if she knew. Perhaps she did. . . .

At ten to four, Tom changed his shirt and combed his hair. When he came out of the barn, he saw that Lonny was already in the truck.

Tom hopped into the pickup beside him.

Lonny wrinkled his nose and sniffed the air. "That you?" he asked.

Tom frowned; maybe he should've taken the time to shower.

"You're wearing cologne," Lonny chided.

Tom's face turned beet-red, and Lonny chuckled. After a moment, Tom smiled, too, and then he made a loud sniffing sound himself. "Hey, I'm not the only one. Who are *you* going to see?"

Lonny's laughter faded quickly enough, and he grumbled an unintelligible reply.

"I'll bet it's Joy Fuller."

Lonny ignored him, and Tom figured he'd better not push the subject. He'd learned to trust Lonny, but he wasn't sure yet how far that trust went. Still, he found he was gradually lowering his guard. Being with Lonny, talking to him about Michelle, had felt good. He enjoyed Letty and Chase, too. Twice now he'd joined the family for Sunday dinner, and those times were about as close as he'd gotten to seeing a real family in action. He hadn't known it could be like that, hadn't realized people related to each other in such a caring and generous manner. Tom was grateful for whatever circumstances had led him to Red Springs and Lonny's barn. It was, without question, the best thing that had happened to him in his whole life.

"Would you mind if I turned on the radio?" Tom asked as a companionable silence grew between them.

"Go ahead."

Tom leaned forward and spun the dial until he found a country-western station. He looked at Lonny, who nodded. Tom relaxed against the seat and before long, his foot was tapping and his hand was bouncing rhythmically on his knee.

Lonny turned the volume up nearly full blast. After only a moment or two, they were both singing at the top of their lungs. Tom was sure anyone passing them on the highway would cringe, because neither of them could sing on key. Tom didn't care, though. This was about as good as it got for someone like him. Cruising down the highway with the windows open, music blaring—and, for this one day, he didn't have a worry in the world other than what kind of flowers to buy his girl for the dance.

The radio was playing at a more discreet volume by the time they reached the outskirts of Red Springs. Lonny pulled up across from Larson's Feed, and Tom opened the passenger door and jumped out.

"I shouldn't be longer than an hour," Lonny told him.

"I'll wait for you here."

With a toot of his horn, Lonny drove off.

Tom jogged across the street and when he walked into the store, Michelle was behind the cash register, smiling at him.

"Hi," she said shyly.

"Hi," Tom answered, having trouble finding his tongue. She was so pretty, it was hard not to just stand there and stare at her.

"Would you like a Coke?" she asked.

"Uh, sure."

"Dad has some in the office. I'll be right back."

"That's fine." He'd wait all day if she asked him to.

Tom leaned against the long counter, then straightened when Michelle's father came in. Tom immediately removed his hat. "Good afternoon, Mr. Larson."

"Tom," the other man said, inclining his head toward him. Then, as if he had important business to attend to, he left almost as suddenly as he'd appeared.

Michelle was back a minute later, holding two cans of soda. "Dad said it'd be okay if the two of us sat out front," she said. The feed store had a porch with two rocking chairs and a big community bulletin board. The porch had weathered with time, and the red-painted building had seen better days, but there was a feeling of comfort here, and even of welcome.

They sat down, and Tom opened his soda and handed it to Michelle. At first she didn't seem to understand that he was opening hers and they needed to exchange cans. When she did, she offered him the biggest, sweetest smile he'd ever seen. Tom thought he'd be willing to open a thousand pop cans for one of her smiles.

"Did you decide about the dance?" she asked, her eyes wide and hopeful.

Tom took his first swallow of Coke, then lowered his head. When he glanced up, he discovered Michelle watching him closely, and she seemed to be holding her breath. He smiled and said, "It looks like I'll be able to go."

Just as he'd anticipated, Michelle nearly exploded with happiness. "You *can?* Really? You're not teasing me, are you?"

He simply shook his head.

She set her pop can aside and pressed her fingers to her lips. "I think I'm going to cry."

"Don't do that," he nearly shouted. Tom didn't know how to respond when a woman cried. Every time he'd seen tears in his mother's eyes, he'd been shaken and scared. And he'd always felt it was his duty to make things right, even though he wasn't the one who'd made her cry.

"I'm just so happy."

"I am, too." Tom wasn't accustomed to this much happiness. He felt he should be on his guard, glance over his shoulder every once in a while, because disappointment probably wasn't far behind.

Michelle picked up her drink. "Thank you," she whispered.

Tom thought *he* should be thanking her. "I need to know what color your dress is," he managed to say instead.

Her lips curved in a smile, and her eyes were alight with joy. "It's pale yellow with little white flowers. I think it's the prettiest dress I've ever seen. I bought it even before I asked you to take me to the dance."

Tom made a mental note of the color. He'd ask Letty what kind of flower he should buy for the corsage. He didn't know much about flowers—or about any of the other things that seemed important to women.

He wouldn't even have known about the corsage if Lonny hadn't casually mentioned it. That'd brought up a flurry of questions on Tom's part. Having never attended a school dance, or any other dance for that matter, he had no idea what to expect. He feared he might inadvertently do or say something embarrassing. He wanted this one night to be as perfect as he could make it. For Michelle, yes, and in a way he could barely understand, for his mother, too.

They sat in silence for a while, and Tom searched for subjects to discuss. His mind whirled with questions and comments.

"The weather will be nice for the carnival and the dance," Michelle said conversationally.

"That's good."

"Dad says not to worry about—" She hesitated and looked away.

Tom frowned, wondering if Michelle's father had said something derogatory about him. "What?" he asked, his heart sinking. He'd barely spoken more than a few words to Mr. Larson. Her father probably didn't need a reason to dislike him, though. Tom had learned early in life that people often didn't. Being poor, being a drunkard's son—those had been reasons enough back home.

"I thought I should tell you."

"Then do it," Tom said, stiffening.

"Kenny's dad phoned mine last Sunday."

Tom didn't like the sound of this. "About what?"

"Mr. Brighton said Kenny's pretty upset about you seeing me. He said he's afraid if you and I go to the dance together, there might be trouble."

Tom relaxed, grateful this situation didn't involve Mr. Larson's feelings toward him. "Kenny Brighton doesn't scare me."

"It bothered my dad. He's afraid Kenny might try to pull something at the dance. Mostly, he doesn't want me to get caught in the middle."

Tom hadn't really considered that. "Your dad's right." He hated to suggest it, but he couldn't see any alternative. "Maybe we'd better not attend the dance."

Michelle's reaction was immediate. "No way are we missing that dance! Not after everything I went through to get you to be my date."

Tom started to protest, but Michelle was adamant. "I'm not going to let Kenny Brighton ruin the last dance of high school. And . . . and you aren't half the man I thought you were if you let him. Besides, Dad and I came to an understanding."

Her words stung Tom's pride. "What do you mean, half the man you thought I was?"

She shook her head. "I didn't mean that part."

He eyed her skeptically.

"Don't you want to know how Dad and I compromised?" she asked, obviously eager to tell him.

"All right."

She smiled again, one of those special smiles that made his heart swell and his throat go dry. "I had to get my mom on my side first, and then the two of us talked to Dad. After a couple of hours, he finally saw reason." She paused long enough to draw in a deep breath. "Dad phoned Lonny last Sunday afternoon and asked him to volunteer as a chaperone for the dance."

Tom had been in the house at the time of the call. So *that* was what this was all about. He scowled darkly. "I don't need anyone to do my fighting for me."

"That's just it, don't you see?" Michelle insisted, her eyes pleading with his for understanding. "If Lonny's at the dance, there won't *be* any fight. Or if there is, he'll make sure it's fair."

Tom wasn't convinced. Kenny and a couple of his friends could come looking for trouble, and if that was the case, Tom wouldn't back down. He didn't want Lonny leaping in to rescue him, either. Tom would take care of the situation, in his own time and his own way.

"Tom?" Michelle whispered.

He tried to reassure her with a smile, but he didn't think it worked, because her expression grew even more distraught. "Don't worry, okay?" he murmured.

"I am, though. You have this . . . this look like you're upset and angry, and it's frightening me."

As much as possible, Tom relaxed. "It'll be fine."

"I shouldn't have said anything."

Tom disagreed. He needed to know what he was up against, so he could come prepared.

Michelle leaned toward him and took his hand, clasping it between both of hers. Her hold was surprisingly strong.

"Look at me," she pleaded.

At first he resisted. He knew he couldn't refuse her, and he wouldn't put himself in a position where he'd be bound by his word.

"Please," she whispered, raising his hand to her lips and kissing his knuckles.

Hot sensation shot up his arm, straight to his heart. Tom closed his eyes rather than get lost in her completely.

"Don't ask me not to fight, Michelle, because I can't

promise you that." His words contained a steely edge as he braced himself against the power she had over him.

"You'll let Lonny chaperone the dance, though, right?"

He nodded. "I can't keep him away."

"That's all I ask, except . . ."

"Except what?"

"Except . . ." She smiled again. "Except that I want you to dance every dance with me."

Now, that was a promise Tom could keep.

Chapter Fifteen

Lonny couldn't stop thinking about his conversation with Joy last Monday afternoon. He'd wanted to tell Letty about it, but hadn't had the chance. What surprised him was the wealth of feeling he'd experienced just seeing her. Perhaps the thought that he might lose her to another man had escalated the intensity of his emotions. He didn't think so, though. These feelings had always been there, hidden by pride, perhaps, but definitely there.

After dropping Tom off at Larson's, he drove over to the school. Joy's car wasn't in the lot. Then he remembered her mentioning something about early dismissal for the rest of the week. That put a dent in his plans. He'd hoped to meet her on the school grounds, figuring they'd be able to talk freely because she'd feel safe in a familiar environment.

He wanted to follow up on their previous conversation. He'd given her a couple of days to contemplate his apology. He hadn't discussed this with his sister, but Lonny felt certain Letty would approve. Lonny was a businessman who preferred to be straightforward and honest in his dealings. He was ready to admit his feelings—feelings he was convinced Joy shared.

Still, he was prepared to go slow, the way Letty had suggested. He needed to earn Joy's trust all over again. But he believed that she knew him, knew the person he really was.

The more Lonny thought about Joy becoming a part of his life—not just for now, but forever—the stronger his desire to make it happen. They'd have a good marriage, he was sure of it, and, if she was willing, he'd like to start a family soon. He wanted the same happiness Chase and Letty had.

Letty was pregnant. Chase had nearly shouted his ear off on Monday night. He'd called after dinner, and when Lonny heard Chase yelling, he'd been afraid some disaster had occurred. It took him a moment to grasp what his friend was telling him—that he was about to become a father and Lonny an uncle for the second time. Apparently Letty had broken the news to Chase over dinner.

Lonny smiled, recalling his reaction. In the same situation, he knew he'd feel exactly the same way. Since he was already at the school, he parked and walked inside, only to find Joy's classroom empty, pretty much as he'd expected.

Lonny tried to decide what to do next. He could always swing by her place, he supposed, climbing back in his truck.

Sure enough, her car was parked on the street in front of her house, and she was in the yard watering her flower beds. She wore denim shorts and a tank top and her feet were bare. The sight of her, dressed so casually, nearly caused him to drive over the curb. She possessed long, shapely legs and the figure he'd once considered skinny made him practically swallow his tongue.

Lonny parked his truck directly behind her Cruiser and turned off the engine. He hesitated, wondering if he should've gotten Letty's advice first. But it was too late now. Joy had seen him.

She stood there glaring at him and holding the hose as if it were a weapon she might use against him.

Lonny got out of the truck and walked over to the sidewalk by her house.

She still clutched the hose, water jetting out, almost daring him to take one step on her green lawn.

"Good afternoon," he said, as politely as he could. He held his hat in his hands, smiling.

"Hello." Her greeting was cool, her tone uninflected. "What are you doing here?"

That was an important question. If he had his way, his answer would be to start the marriage negotiations. . . . Well, perhaps *negotiations* wasn't quite the right word. He'd broach the subject directly—except he knew Letty would tell him that was a mistake.

"I stopped by to see how your day went," he

answered, hoping he looked relaxed.

"Why?" she asked bluntly, raising the hose. He was just outside the line of fire—or water.

"Put the hose down, Joy."

She slowly lowered it, pointing it at the ground. "Why are you here?" she demanded again. Despite her hostility, her eyes told him she was pleased he'd come to see her.

"Wait," he said. He ran to his truck and grabbed a large bunch of wildflowers from the passenger seat. He'd picked them by the side of the road; there were yellow ones and blue ones and some pink and white ones, too. He didn't have a vase, so he'd wrapped the stems in a plastic bag with water.

Joy looked as if she didn't know what to say. In the months they'd dated, he'd never brought her flowers.

She was speechless for a long moment. "That was a lovely thing to do." She almost managed a smile—almost.

Joy set the hose on the lawn and hurried to the side of the house to turn off the water. Then she returned to accept his flowers and tucked them in the crook of her arm.

The silence stretched between them.

Feeling naked without his hat, Lonny set it back on his head. "I went to see you at school."

"My last parent-teacher appointment was over by two," she explained.

He nodded.

More silence.

She wasn't in a talkative mood, and Lonny recalled his sister's advice about going slow. Hard as it was to walk away, he decided he had to. "I hope you enjoy the flowers," he mumbled, trying to hide his disappointment.

Joy offered him a tentative smile. "Would you care for a glass of iced tea?" she asked in a friendly voice.

"Sure." He tried to sound nonchalant but was secretly delighted. This, finally, was progress. "That would be nice. I'd also like your opinion on something if you don't mind." He had an idea for supplementing his and Chase's income and genuinely wanted to hear what she thought. She had the advantage of living in a ranching community, while having a big-city background, both of which were relevant to his plan. He'd like her advice on how to help Tom, too.

"All right." Joy led the way into her duplex, to the kitchen. The sliding glass door opened onto a patio, which she'd edged with large containers holding a variety of flowers. She retrieved a large jar and arranged the wildflowers—some of which were probably weeds, he thought, slightly embarrassed as he compared them to her array of plants. After filling their glasses, she suggested they enjoy their tea outside.

Lonny held open the sliding glass door and followed her outside. Discussing this idea with her had been a spur-of-the-moment thing. But he sensed that Joy would have a valuable perspective he should hear before he approached Chase and Letty with his suggestion.

He sipped his tea and set the tall glass on the patio table. "I figure by now you've learned something about raising cattle," he began.

"A little," she agreed.

Lonny nodded encouragingly.

"I know you and Chase raise grass-fed cattle versus taking your herd to a feedlot," she continued.

"Right," he said, impressed by her understanding. "Basically, that means the animal's main diet is grass. We supplement it with some other roughage, otherwise there can be problems. Our cattle are leaner and the beef has less saturated fat."

"I think that's admirable."

"The thing is, the economics of ranching, especially with a small herd, just doesn't work anymore. Chase and I are just too ornery to admit it." He smiled as he said that. "I suffer from an unfortunate streak of stubbornness, as you already know." He let those words sink in, so she'd realize again how much he regretted their past differences. "Now that Letty's pregnant, Chase is worried. He sold off a large chunk of his land. When he did, he figured on buying it back one day, but the truth is, that doesn't seem possible now." Lonny wasn't sure Chase had admitted that even to himself.

"What are you going to do?" Joy asked, sounding concerned.

"I've been giving this a lot of thought. I could always let Tom go. As it is, I'm not paying him a living wage— I can't afford to. It's hard just to make enough to keep the ranch going." Granted, Lonny still had some savings from his rodeo days, although he'd invested most of that cash in buying their herd.

"Have you considered selling?"

That was probably a solution he *should* consider, but no matter how bad the situation got, he couldn't see himself doing it. "Ranching is more than an occupation—and selling isn't really an option, at least not for me and Chase. This land came to us through our families. It's our inheritance and what we hope to pass on to our children and their children. It's more than land." He didn't know if Joy would understand this part. She hadn't been born into ranching the way he and Chase and Letty had. Perhaps he'd been wrong to bring up the subject. He felt foolish now, uncertain. This wasn't all that different from declaring his feelings for her—and proposing marriage. At least now, she'd know what she was getting when he did ask. If she said yes . . .

"You said you've got an idea. Does it have to do with this?"

"Yeah. I haven't talked to anyone else about it and, well, it's pretty much off the top of my head."

"Go on," she urged.

"I was looking through a magazine the other day and came across an article about guest ranches. I guess they used to be called dude ranches, and according to this article they're more popular than ever. The owners put people up for maybe a week and take them on cattle drives and so on. I nearly fell off my chair when I saw what they were charging."

Joy frowned thoughtfully. "I've heard of them. Like

in that movie *City Slickers*? It came out in the mid-nineties. I really enjoyed it."

"So did I, and the rest of us in town, too. I'm not laughing now, though."

Joy raised her hand. "Do you mean to say—are you actually thinking of taking on a bunch of . . . city slickers?"

He ducked one shoulder. "I am. I don't have a bunkhouse, but Chase does, and his ranch is right next to mine. It seems there are people out there willing to pay top dollar for the experience of working with cattle."

"Sounds promising," Joy said. "How much would it add to your workload?"

"For now, the brunt of the operation would fall on Chase and Letty because they have the facilities to put up folks and I don't." He paused. "The whole idea is still in its infancy."

"For that kind of enterprise, you'd need to have a sociable personality. Which you do. You get along well with people," she said, then added, "with a few exceptions."

He smiled because he knew she was talking about the two of them. "I generally don't have a problem," he said, "unless I let my pride stand in the way."

"You're not the only one with that problem."

In other words, Joy was acknowledging her part in their falling out.

"What do you think?" he asked eagerly. He hadn't used this as a ploy to get her to confess her own failings;

that wasn't the point. As far as he was concerned, the past was the past, and this was now. They sat on her patio, two friends sharing ideas.

"You'd have to advertise," she said, "when you're ready to launch this."

"We're going to need a whole lot of planning before we can go ahead, but like I said, I've just started thinking about this."

Joy beamed at him. "I love it. I really do."

He smiled back, even more excited about the guest ranch idea. He couldn't explain why, but it'd seemed right—natural—to discuss it with Joy first.

"I'd like to bring Tom in on the deal, too," he said, "but only in the summers when he's out of school. That's something I want to talk to you about later."

"Tom's still in school?"

"No, but I hope he'll go to college. We've been looking at scholarships on-line, and he's already applied for a few in the state. He's definitely got the brains and the drive."

"What about his family?"

Lonny brushed off the question. The truth was, he still didn't know much about Tom's family other than that his mother was dead and his father was a drunk—facts Tom had only recently, and reluctantly, divulged. "He doesn't have any."

"So you're helping him?"

"I'm trying to. Tom deserves a break in life."

"I think you're doing a wonderful thing. And I'd be happy to help in any way I can."

171

"Thanks." Her praise flustered him. "Getting back to the guest ranch . . ."

She glanced away. "Letty's a fabulous cook. I imagine part of the attraction would be the meals."

"I'd want to appeal to families," Lonny said, throwing out another idea.

"You'll need activities for children, then," Joy said.

"Yeah." Lonny was glad she'd followed his thought to its logical conclusion.

"I'd be able to help you with that," she added. "I could write out a list of suggestions."

That was precisely what he'd wanted to hear. "Great!" He could see that she was catching his enthusiasm.

"Did you check to see if there are other guest ranches in the area?"

"I did. There are a few in different parts of the state, but there aren't any within a hundred miles of Red Springs." Nor were there any operated by former rodeo champions.

Their eyes met, and Lonny realized they were smiling at each other. Again. Really smiling. "I'd appreciate any help you could give us," Lonny said, forcing himself to look away. He could feel his pulse quickening, and it didn't have anything to do with his excitement about the guest ranch, either.

"If you'll excuse me a moment," Joy said abruptly, "I—I'll get us refills on the tea."

"Sure."

She stood as if she was in a rush and Lonny wondered

if he'd said or done something to offend her. On impulse, he downed the last of his tea and hurried inside.

The darkness of her kitchen, after the sunlight outside, momentarily blinded him. When he could focus, he found Joy standing by the sink with her back to him. Letty would be pretty mad if she knew what he was thinking just then. Regardless, Lonny walked up behind Joy and placed his hands lightly on her shoulders.

His heart reacted wildly when she leaned against him, and Lonny breathed in the clean, warm scent of her hair.

"Don't be angry with me," he whispered close to her ear.

"Angry? Why?" she whispered back.

"I want to kiss you again."

She released a soft indefinable moan. Then she turned and locked her arms around his neck. A moment later, his mouth was on hers with a hunger and a need that threatened to overwhelm him. Arms about her waist, he lifted her from the floor and devoured her mouth with his. He couldn't take enough or give enough.

When she tore her mouth from his, he immediately dropped his arms and stepped away, fearing she'd rant at him like she had before, when he'd kissed her in the parking lot.

She didn't.

Instead, she stared up at him with a shocked expression. She'd leaned one arm against the counter as if she needed to maintain her balance, and held her free hand over her heart.

Lonny waited. He couldn't even begin to predict what she'd say or do next.

"I . . . I—thank you for the f-flowers," she stammered. "They're l-lovely."

"Can I take you to dinner?" he asked, not wanting to leave.

She blinked slowly, as if she'd needed a moment to decipher the question. "It's a little early, isn't it?"

"An early dinner, then." He was finding it difficult to remember Letty's advice about going slow.

She didn't answer for a long time. "Not tonight."

Lonny swallowed his disappointment and nodded. "I guess I'll be going."

"Okay."

Joy walked him to the front door and held open the screen. "Thank you for stopping by."

He touched the brim of his hat and left. But as he approached his truck, his steps grew heavier. He'd completely forgotten about Josh! But then he brightened. Judging by the way she'd kissed him, Joy had, too.

Chapter Sixteen

"Stupid, stupid, stupid!" Joy wanted to bang her head against the wall in frustration. Not only had she invited Lonny Ellison into her home, she'd allowed him to kiss her. *Again.* Worse, she'd practically *begged* him to kiss her. Then, to complicate matters even more, she'd kissed him back. The man made her crazy and here she was, kissing him with an abandon that had left her nerves tingling. Instead of avoiding him, she was encouraging him.

One hand against her forehead, Joy closed the front door and, for good measure, emphatically turned the lock. She didn't know if she was keeping Lonny out or keeping herself from running after him.

This was a disaster! Josh was due in two days. Two days. Because of their e-mails and telephone conversations, he was coming with the expectation of resuming their relationship.

Josh was perfect for her. His future was secure, he was handsome and congenial. They had a lot in common and their parents were good friends. At one time, he was everything she'd ever wanted in a man.

At one time—what was she thinking? She'd broken up with Lonny almost two years ago, after a relationship that had barely lasted three months. The fact that he was back in her life now could only be described as bad timing. She didn't want him to invade her every waking moment—or to take up residence in her dreams, as he'd begun to do.

Totally confused about her feelings toward Lonny, Joy returned to the kitchen and rearranged the wildflowers in their vase. She was touched by the image of him scrambling in ditches to collect them; it was quite possibly the sweetest gesture she'd ever received from a man. Anyone could call a florist and read off a credit card number, she told herself; not every man would go and pick his own flowers.

When she'd finished, Joy set the bouquet in the center of her kitchen table and stepped back to admire the flowers. Lonny was proud and stubborn, but he'd let her know he was sorry about what had happened two years earlier.

"The jerk," she muttered. "He did that on purpose."

The doorbell rang and Joy went rigid. If it was Lonny again, she didn't want him seeing her like this. She was an emotional mess. And even though she preferred to blame him for that, she knew she couldn't.

"Who is it?" she called out.

"Petal Pushers," Jerry Hawkins shouted back.

The local florist shop! Surprised, Joy unlatched the dead bolt and threw open the door to discover Jerry standing on the front step, holding a lovely floral arrangement protected by cellophane. "Mom asked me to drop these by," he explained.

Sally owned the shop and her son made deliveries after school.

"Who'd be sending me flowers?" Joy asked. Considering her previous thoughts, she was all too conscious of the irony.

"Mom said they're from a man."

Joy's eyes widened as she accepted the arrangement. It consisted of pink lilies, bright yellow African daisies, sweet Williams and gladioli, interspersed with greenery and beautifully displayed in an old-fashioned watering can.

"Do I need to sign anything?" she asked.

"No," Jerry was quick to tell her. "Enjoy."

"I will, thank you." She closed the door with her foot and carried the large arrangement into the kitchen, placing it on the counter. As she unpinned the card from the bright yellow ribbon, she shook her head. The flowers had to be from Josh.

She was right. The card read: *I'm looking forward to this weekend. Josh.*

Until that very afternoon, Joy had been looking forward to seeing him, too. No—she still was, but not with the same unalloyed pleasure. She put the formal arrangement next to the glass jar filled with the wildflowers Lonny had brought her. Once again, the irony didn't escape her. Businessman and rancher. One as polished and smooth as the satin ribbon wrapped about the watering can and the other as unsophisticated as . . . the plastic grocery bag in which he'd presented his flowers.

These were the two men in her life. They didn't know it, but they were fast coming to a showdown. Josh would arrive for the school carnival and, sure as anything, Lonny would be in town at the same time. Already her stomach was in knots. Joy had no idea what to do; the only person she could talk to was Letty.

She waited until she'd calmed down before she reached for the phone and hit speed dial to connect with Letty, who answered on the first ring.

"Joy, it's so good to hear from you," she said enthusiastically.

"Can you talk for a minute?" Joy asked, too unnerved to bother with the normal pleasantries.

"Of course." Letty's voice was concerned. "Is everything all right?"

"No . . . I don't know," she mumbled before blurting out, "Lonny came by earlier."

Letty's hesitation was long enough for Joy to notice.

"He brought me a bouquet of wildflowers and, Letty, it was just so sweet of him."

"Lonny brought you flowers," Letty repeated, as if she had trouble believing it herself. "Really?"

"Yes. I'm looking at them right now." She didn't mention the second bouquet she was looking at, too. Sighing, Joy sank into a kitchen chair and rested her elbow on the table. She supported her forehead with one hand as she closed her eyes, suddenly feeling tired. "I should've told him Josh was coming. I wanted to, but I didn't." Granted, it would've been a bit awkward when she was in his arms kissing him. *Not* that she planned to mention that scene in the kitchen.

"Joy," her friend gently chastised, "don't you realize how much my brother cares about you?"

She swallowed hard because she did know and it distressed her. "I sort of guessed. . . . The last couple of times we've met, he's been so cordial and polite. He's even told me how sorry he feels about our disagreement, and I never thought he'd do anything like that."

Letty released a deep sigh and said in a soft voice, "I

didn't, either. Oh dear, I feel wretched."

Joy's eyes flew open. "Is it the pregnancy?"

"I'm perfectly healthy. This has to do with Lonny. He
. . . asked for my help."

"Your help in what?" Joy was already confused and
this wasn't making things any easier.

"My brother asked for my advice on how to win you
back. If you must know, I was the one who suggested
he bring you flowers."

"Oh."

"It took that near-accident to make Lonny see the
truth. He's always cared about you, only he was too
stubborn to admit it. Now it's hitting him between the
eyes. Josh wants you back, too, and you're going to
have to make a decision. Either way, someone's going
to be disappointed."

"You're right."

Silence fell between them as they both mulled over
the significance of this. Letty spoke first.

"Listen, Joy, you're my friend but Lonny's my
brother, and I don't think I'm the best person to be
talking to about this," she said.

"There isn't anyone else," Joy cried. "Letty, please,
just hear me out?"

"I'll try, but you need to know I'm not exactly a neu-
tral observer. It's a mess," she said, "and to some extent
I blame myself."

"You didn't do anything."

"I did, though," Letty confessed, sounding thor-
oughly miserable. "I encouraged Lonny, built up the

idea of a relationship with you. You know I think the world of you and in my enthusiasm—well, never mind. None of that's important now."

"I feel terrible," Joy murmured. "Just terrible."

"Do you still have feelings for my brother?" Letty asked, her voice elevated with what sounded like hope.

That was the million-dollar question. "I . . . I'm not sure." At the moment, Joy was too bewildered to know how she felt about either man.

"Okay, fair enough," Letty said, exhaling a lengthy sigh.

"The thing is, Josh is coming this weekend."

"Believe me, I'm well aware of that," Letty muttered.

Joy pressed the phone harder against her ear. "I don't want any trouble."

"What do you mean?"

"Lonny's going to the carnival, isn't he?"

"Of course."

"Is there any way you could distract him?" Joy pleaded. "Keep him away until after Josh leaves?" As soon as she said the words, she realized how ridiculous that sounded—as if these two men were a couple of bulls or stallions that had to be separated to prevent a dangerous confrontation.

Letty gave a short, cheerless laugh. "Lonny won't cause any trouble, if that's what you're thinking," she assured Joy. "That's not his style. Besides, he already knows."

"Lonny knows? About Josh?"

"Yes, I told him."

Involuntarily her foot started tapping. "That explains it, then."

"Explains what?"

"The flowers, the apology, everything." So Josh's pending visit was the reason for Lonny's abrupt change in behavior.

"You're wrong," Letty said. "He came to talk to me before he knew about Josh."

"He did?" That didn't really improve the situation; however, at least it cleared up his motives. "Oh, dear."

"What?" Letty asked.

"Nothing. Just . . . he has a wonderful idea for the ranch. He wanted to hear my opinion before he brought it to you and Chase. I think it's brilliant."

"What is it?"

"I can't tell you. Lonny will when he's ready. I like it, though, I really do. I even told him I'd be willing to help. I was sincere about that." However, if her relationship with Josh progressed the way she'd once hoped, that would be impossible. For the first time since he'd contacted her, Joy regretted that he was coming to Red Springs. His timing couldn't have been worse—or better. The problem was, she couldn't decide which.

Letty added, "Don't hurt my brother, Joy. He might be the most stubborn man you've ever met in your life, but he's decent and hardworking and he genuinely cares for you."

"I know," Joy said, and she meant it. "I'll talk to him tomorrow." She needed time to work out what to say, and yet, no matter how prepared she was, this would be one of the most difficult conversations she'd ever had.

Chapter Seventeen

The next evening, Lonny reflected that his day had gone very well indeed. He'd awakened in a fine mood and it was still with him. He felt inspired, motivated and challenged, all at once. His goal was to win Joy's heart, and he believed he'd made some strides toward it. He wasn't going to let some fast-talking businessman steal her away, even if he was an old boyfriend. Lonny didn't know exactly what Josh did for a living but picturing him as some high-and-mighty company mogul suited his purposes.

Joy loved *him*. She might not realize it yet, but she would soon. His mission was to convince her that she belonged right here in Red Springs—with him.

Lonny hadn't fully appreciated his sister's dating advice until yesterday. Those wildflowers had worked better than he'd ever imagined they would. He could almost see Joy's heart melt the instant she laid eyes on that bunch of flowers.

After dinner, feeling good about life in general, Lonny sat out on his porch, in the rocking chair that had once been his father's. He couldn't remember the last time he'd lazed away an evening there. He sometimes joined Letty and Chase on the porch over at their place, but he seldom sat here on his own. Music sounded faintly from inside the barn, where Tom was practicing his dance moves. Given all the time and effort the boy had put into preparing for this dance, he should be pretty confident.

Lonny relaxed and linked his fingers behind his head. He was feeling downright domestic. He'd waited nearly thirty-five years to consider marriage. He hadn't been in any rush to settle down, because marriage meant responsibilities, and he already had enough of those.

Funny, he didn't think like that anymore. He was actually looking forward to living the rest of his life with Joy. Marriage to her was bound to be interesting, not to mention passionate and satisfying in every conceivable way.

So far, his sister's advice to "go slow" had been right on the money. Come Friday, he'd be in town for the carnival and later the dance. He could visualize it now. By this time tomorrow night, he'd be holding her hand and later he'd be dancing with her, and that was all it would take to tell everyone in Red Springs how he felt about Joy Fuller.

A cloud of swirling dust alerted him to the fact that there was a car coming down the long driveway. Lonny stood, and when he did, Joy's PT Cruiser came into view. A sensation of happiness stole over him. The last person he'd expected to see here, at his place, was Joy, and at the same time, she was the one person he most wanted it to be.

He'd hurried down the steps and was walking across the yard as she parked. At that moment, Tom stuck his head out of the barn. He smiled at Lonny and gave him a thumbs-up, then returned to his practicing.

Lonny greeted Joy from halfway across the yard. "This is a pleasant surprise."

Her eyes didn't quite meet his. "Would it be all right if we talked?"

"It would be more than all right." He placed his hand at the small of her back and steered her toward the porch. "My parents used to sit out here in the evenings. I'd consider it an honor to have you join me." He hoped she picked up on his subtle hint about the two of them sitting together in the space once reserved for a long-married couple. . . .

Lonny reached for the second rocking chair and dragged it closer to his own. "Can I get you anything? A pillow? Something to drink?" he asked, minding his manners in a way that would've made his mother proud.

"Nothing, thanks," she said before sitting down.

She seemed nervous, but Lonny wanted her to know there wasn't any reason to be. He sat next to her and they both rocked for a few minutes.

"It's quite a coincidence that you should stop by," he commented casually. "I was just thinking about you."

"You were?"

"Yup, I spent most of my day thinking about you." He'd dreamed about her, too, and awakened with the warmest, most delicious feeling. He couldn't recall

184

everything his dream had entailed, but he remembered the gist of it—they were married and there were three youngsters running around. Two boys and a cute little girl. He was feeding the youngest in a high chair, while Joy was busy getting dinner on the table for the rest of the family. He'd felt as if his heart might burst with happiness—and then the alarm woke him.

"Lonny, please just listen."

She sounded so serious now, and that wasn't like her.

"I'll listen to anything you want to tell me," he said, matching the seriousness of her expression.

She closed her eyes and kept them tightly shut. Lonny turned his chair so they sat facing each other, their knees touching. He took both of her hands and held them in his.

"Joy?" he asked. "What's wrong?"

She opened her eyes and gave him a tentative smile. "You know Josh Howell's coming to town, don't you?"

He nodded. "Letty mentioned it." He didn't care. Joy loved him—didn't she?—and he loved her. As far as he was concerned, the other man was a minor inconvenience.

"But—"

Rather than listen to her extol Josh's virtues, or even say his name, he leaned forward and gently pressed his lips to hers. Her mouth softened and instantly molded and shaped to his, as if she wanted this as badly as he did. Cradling the back of her neck, he deepened the kiss. The tantalizing sensations tormented and delighted him. Joy, too, he guessed, because after a moment, she twisted her head away, breaking the contact.

"I want to talk to you and you're making it impossible," she moaned.

"Good." He wanted her as caught up in this whirlwind of feeling as he was. More important, he wanted her to understand that they were meant to be together, the two of them. Josh might be her past, but he was her future.

"Please, Lonny, just listen, all right?"

"If you insist." But then he brought his lips back to hers. This second round was even more delectable than the first. . . .

"Please. I can't think when you're kissing me," she pleaded, and seemed to have difficulty breathing normally.

She wasn't the only one. "It's hard to refuse you anything, but I don't know if I can stop."

"Try. For the sake of my sanity, would you kindly try?"

He pushed his chair back and motioned for her to stand. When she did, his arms circled her waist and he pulled her into his lap. Her eyes widened with surprise. She hardly seemed aware that her arms had slipped around his neck. She stared at him. "Why did you do that?"

"Isn't it obvious?" He longed to have her close, needed her close. She must know how deeply their kisses had affected him.

"I have something important to tell you," she said

but without the conviction of earlier.

"Okay," he murmured as he spread soft kisses down the side of her neck. She sighed and inclined her head. Apparently what she had to tell him wasn't that important, after all.

"I've reached a decision. . . ." Her voice held a soft, beseeching quality.

A sense of exhilaration and triumph shot through him. "Okay, no kissing for . . ." He checked his watch. "Five minutes, and then all bets are off." He returned his mouth to the hollow of her throat, savoring the feel of her smooth skin. With each foray she melted a little more in his embrace.

Joy moved her head to one side. "That's kissing," she said breathlessly.

"I'm staying clear of your lips. Tell me what's so important that you had to drive all the way out here."

She caught his earlobe between her teeth. Hot sensation coursed through him like a powerful electric shock. This was torture, and she was quickly driving him beyond reason. In self-defense, he seized her by the waist. To his surprise, his hands came upon bare flesh. Her light sweater had ridden up just enough to reveal her midriff. Her skin felt so smooth, so warm. . . . He'd never intended to take things this far, but now there was no stopping him. He slid his hand higher and cupped her breast. As his palm closed around it, he heard her soft intake of breath. The fastening of her bra, which was in front, seemed to spring open of its own accord, spilling her breast into his waiting palm.

Joy buried her face in his neck and took several deep breaths. His own breathing had grown labored.

"You keep doing that and I'm going to embarrass us both," he said.

She instantly went still.

"Joy," he said, although he found it difficult to speak at all. "I don't care why you're here or what you came to tell me. I love—"

She brought her index finger to his lips. "Don't say it." Pain flashed from her eyes.

"Okay." He sobered. "I think you'd better explain." He made an effort to focus on her words.

"Josh Howell is coming tomorrow," she said.

"Yes, I know. We talked about that. I'm not worried."

"I've decided not to renew my teaching contract. I'm moving back to the Puget Sound area."

A sense of unreality gripped him. He blinked. "What?"

"I—I've decided not to renew my teaching contract."

When the words did sink in, he stared into her eyes, but she couldn't hold his gaze.

"Say something," she pleaded. "Don't look at me like—like you don't believe I'll do it. I've made my decision."

"Okay," he said, his thoughts chaotic. "The decision is yours to make. I don't want you to go, but I can't kidnap you and keep you in the root cellar until you change your mind."

She frowned unhappily. "I know this upsets you. I haven't told anyone else yet. I wanted to tell you first."

"Any particular reason you're confiding in me?"

She nodded several times. "Considering everything that's happened, I felt I should."

"So you're in love with Josh?"

Joy bit her lip. "I don't know."

"But you've already decided you're leaving with him?" Lonny asked, not understanding her logic. Joy didn't seem to notice that he was caressing her back with one hand and cupping her breast with the other.

"I won't leave right away."

"Of course," he agreed quietly.

"Josh and I . . . we've been talking and e-mailing and—" She let the rest fade.

"Renewing your acquaintance," he finished.

"Exactly." Her eyes were half-closed as she spoke.

"And you're thinking that because of Josh, you'll leave Red Springs?"

"Yes." Slowly exhaling, she looked directly at him. "The thing is, I hate to go."

"The town will miss you. So will I."

"I'll miss you, too," she whispered.

It was exactly what Lonny had hoped to hear. "Then don't go."

She didn't respond.

"I'm hoping you'll reconsider."

"I . . . I don't think I can."

"If you stay here, we could get married," he suggested.

Apparently he'd shocked her into speechlessness. "I've been doing a lot of thinking about what went wrong with our relationship earlier," he said, "and I realize now I was the problem."

"You?"

"It was my fault. I reacted the same way then as I did when we had the traffic accident—I mean incident."

"You were unreasonable and high-handed and—"

He stopped her before she could continue with the list of his faults. "I love you, Joy, and I don't want you to move away."

She scrambled off his lap, nearly stumbling in her eagerness to get off the porch. "You're trying to confuse me!"

"No. I'm telling you right now, it'd be a big mistake to make such an important decision while you're unsure of what you want. That's what I did, and it cost me two good years I might've spent with you."

"I . . . I've already made up my mind."

She was fighting herself just as hard as she was fighting him. He longed to kiss her again, but he knew that would only infuriate her.

"I'm . . . l-leaving," she said, stuttering as she turned away. "I can see it wasn't a good idea to talk to you about this."

He didn't make a move to stop her. "You might want to fasten your bra before you go," he said in a reasonable tone.

Embarrassed and flustered, she whirled around and fumbled with her clothes.

It occurred to Lonny that she might have expected a different reaction to her announcement. "Do you want me to be jealous?" he asked. He was prepared to act as if he was, and it wouldn't be that big a stretch. He'd never even met Josh Howell, but he didn't like the man.

"No!" she blurted out irritably.

"Good. Because I will if that's what you want. But truth be told, I'm more confident than ever that we're meant to be together." He smiled at her. "Like I said, we've already lost two years and I'm not planning to repeat that mistake. I hope you aren't, either. We're not getting any younger, you know, and if we're going to have kids . . ."

That really seemed to upset her, because her eyes went wide with shock. At least, he hoped it was shock and not horror.

"Joy," he said, staying calm and clearheaded. "We were pretty involved physically just a few minutes ago. I can't believe you'd allow a man to kiss you and touch you the way I just did if you didn't have strong feelings for him."

She backed away. "Josh will be here tomorrow, and all I ask is that you leave us alone."

He shrugged. "I'm not making any promises. You'd feel the same if some other gal was stepping in and trying to steal me away."

"I'm not a prize to be won at the carnival. You're so sure of yourself! I should marry Josh just to spite you."

That was an empty threat if he'd ever heard one. "You won't."

She made an exasperated sound and marched down the porch steps, almost tripping in her haste.

"Joy," he said, following her. "I don't want you to leave when you're this upset."

"I have to go!"

"I love you. If you want, I'll be furious and jealous and I'll corner Josh Howell and demand that he get outta town."

She shook her head vigorously. "Don't you dare!"

"I'm serious. I'm not willing to lose you to Josh."

"You've already lost me. I came here to tell you I'm not renewing my teaching contract."

Rather than argue with her, he sighed heavily. "Kiss me goodbye."

That seemed to fluster her more than anything else he'd said. "No!"

"Joy, my parents never went to sleep without settling an argument. That's the advice they always gave newly married couples. I don't want us to get in the habit of parting angry, either."

Aghast, she glared at him. "But we're not a couple!"

"But I believe we *should* be a couple. Because I love you and I know you love me."

It looked as if she was about to burst into tears. "No, I don't. I refuse to love anyone as stubborn . . . and—"

"Pigheaded," he supplied.

Climbing into the car, she insisted one final time, "I don't love you!" She slammed the door shut and started the engine. A moment later, she tore out of the yard, kicking up a trail of dust.

"Oh, yes, you do," Lonny whispered. "You do love me, Joy Fuller. And I'm going to prove it."

Chapter Eighteen

After the confrontation with Lonny, Joy barely slept that night. The man's arrogance was unbelievable. How dared he insist she was in love with him!

It'd seemed only right that she tell Lonny about her decision. Going to him had been a mistake, though, one that made her question her own sanity. He'd been condescending, and treated her as if she was too feeble-minded to form her own opinions. He'd practically laughed at her! Mortified, Joy wanted to bury her face in her hands.

She'd thought . . . well, she'd hoped they could part as friends. That was what she'd wanted to tell him. Instead, she'd ended their conversation feeling angry and uncertain. To be fair, she had to admit there was a certain physical attraction between them. But that was his fault, not hers. Well, it wasn't really a question of *fault,* she supposed. The man could kiss like no one she'd ever known. So of course she'd kissed him back; any red-blooded woman would.

She got out of bed, yawning, unable to stop thinking about last night. Just remembering the way he'd pulled her into his lap, and then proceeded to seduce her, had her cheeks burning with embarrassment. As she readied for school, she chose her pink pantsuit. Today was the biggest event of the year in Red Springs. Her eyes already burned from lack of sleep and it was going to be a long, long day. First, the carnival, then the high school dance. On top of all that, Josh would show up sometime around four—just when everything was getting started. If she could make it through today without losing her mind or breaking into tears, it would be a miracle.

The last day of school was more of a formality than an occasion to teach. The students were restless and anxious to escape from the moment the bus dropped them off. It was a bittersweet experience for Joy to see her students move on to the next grade. Each one was special to her. Most of the third-graders would be back in this classroom next year as fourth-grade students, and there'd be a group of new, younger kids, as well.

At noon, the bell rang and her pupils dashed out the door, shouting with excitement and glee.

Smiling, Joy walked onto the playground to wave goodbye, thinking this might be her last opportunity. The contract sat at home unsigned. Even now, she wasn't sure what to do. She'd made her decision and then Lonny had kissed her and all at once her certainty had evaporated.

The school buses had already lined up, their diesel engines running. The children formed straggling rows and boarded the buses with far more noise than usual. Most would return with their families for the carnival in a few hours.

As Joy grinned and waved and called out goodbyes, she reflected that her afternoon would be busy, getting everything done before Josh arrived. She'd made a reservation for him at the one and only local motel, the

Rest Easy Inn. When she saw Josh, she told herself, she'd know her own feelings, know what was right for her. Joy couldn't help wondering what this weekend would hold for them both. She wished . . . Her thoughts came to a dead halt. What *did* she wish?

If Josh had contacted her a few months earlier, everything would be different, and yet the only real change in her life was resuming her relationship with Lonny.

"Goodbye, Miss Fuller," Cricket said, coming up to Joy and throwing both arms around her waist.

"I'll see you later, won't I?" Joy asked, crouching beside the little girl.

"Oh, yes," Cricket said. "I'm going to ride the Ferris wheel with my daddy, and he said he'd buy me a snow cone and popcorn and cotton candy, too."

"I'll roll you an extra-big cotton candy," Joy promised.

An unfamiliar vehicle pulled into the parking lot. Ever wary of strangers, Joy narrowed her eyes suspiciously. Then the car door opened and a man stepped out.

"Josh," Joy whispered. He was early—and every bit as handsome as she remembered.

He gazed around as though he wasn't sure where to go. Staring at him, Joy was again struck by his good looks. She'd been afraid he couldn't possibly live up to her memories—or her expectations. Wrong. He was even *more* attractive now. More everything. He exuded success and ambition.

Joy began walking toward him. "Josh!" She raised her arm high above her head.

As soon as Josh saw her, he smiled broadly and strode toward her. Then they were standing face-to-face and after a moment of just staring at each other, they hugged. It was so good to see him.

"Hey, let me take a look at you," Josh said, holding her at arm's length. "You've changed," he said, his bright blue eyes meeting hers. "You're more beautiful than ever."

His words embarrassed her a little and she laughed. "I was just thinking the same about you."

"Miss Fuller, Miss Fuller," Cricket said. She'd trailed behind Joy and now stood there, her eyes as round as pie tins.

"Yes, Cricket?" Joy said, turning away from Josh to focus her attention on the child. "What is it?"

"Who is this man?" Cricket asked, with uncharacteristic rudeness.

"This is my friend, Mr. Howell."

Cricket frowned.

"Mr. Howell drove to Red Springs to visit me," Joy elaborated.

"Is he your *boy*friend?" she asked.

Before Joy could answer, Josh did. "Yes, I'm Miss Fuller's boyfriend." He slipped his arm around Joy's waist and brought her close to his side.

The girl's lower lip shot out. "I'm telling my Uncle Lonny." Having made that announcement, Cricket stomped off the playground and boarded the school bus, the last child to do so.

"And just who is Cricket's Uncle Lonny?" Josh asked, quirking his eyebrow at her.

"A local rancher," Joy said, not inclined to explain if she didn't have to.

"Really?" Josh didn't sound too concerned, which pleased Joy. She didn't want him to worry. And there was no reason for him to be jealous. . . .

"Did you tell me about 'Uncle' Lonny?" he asked.

"I'm sure I did," Joy said in casual tones. "He owns a ranch about twenty minutes outside town."

"He's not the one you had the near-collision with, is he?"

"Yes," she cried, surprised Josh had remembered. "That's Lonny. We dated for a while when I first moved to Red Springs—I know I mentioned that in my e-mails—but we broke up and I haven't had much to do with him since." Because it was bound to happen at some point this evening, she added, "You'll meet him later." She dreaded the prospect, but there was no help for it. Her only hope was that Lonny would ignore both her and Josh, unlikely though that seemed.

"Is your rancher friend still being unreasonable about the accident?" Josh asked.

"Actually, he's been pretty decent about it lately. He said I should just forget the whole thing."

"And you have?"

She nodded, more than eager to get off the subject of Lonny. Taking Josh's hand, she smiled up at him. "Let me finish a few things at school and then maybe we could go to lunch."

"Sure. In the meantime, I'll check into the motel."

"Okay." Releasing his hand, she nodded again. She hadn't expected Josh this soon and she still had loose ends to tie up in her classroom. All the arrangements were in place for tonight. When Letty had learned Josh would be coming, she'd volunteered to take the second half of Joy's shift so she'd have a chance to be with her visitor. From her past experience with the cotton candy machine, Joy knew she'd need time to clean up before the dance, too.

"There's a nice Mexican restaurant on Main Street," she suggested. "I could meet you there in an hour."

"Perfect."

Hands on his hips, Josh looked over at the school. "This is a rather quaint building, isn't it?"

Joy had thought the same thing when she'd first seen the stone schoolhouse, built fifty years earlier, but she'd grown used to it. The school felt comfortable to her, and it evoked an enjoyable nostalgia.

"I love it," she said fondly. They just didn't build schools like this anymore, and while the budget called for a new schoolhouse two years from now, Joy would miss this one. Although, of course, it didn't matter because she wouldn't be here.

Josh nodded sympathetically, as if he understood her feelings. "I'll see you in an hour, then."

Joy felt light and carefree as she returned to her classroom. She intended to go into this new relationship with

Josh wholeheartedly, see where it led. Deep down, though, Joy suspected neither one of them was ready for marriage. Still, she wanted to make this work. The fly in the ointment, as her grandmother would've put it, was Lonny Ellison. He arrogantly claimed she was in love with him and . . . he might not be wrong. Or not completely. But that certainly didn't mean a long-term relationship between them would succeed.

By the time Joy hurried into the restaurant, she was ten minutes later than she'd planned. She'd left several duties unfinished, which meant she'd have to go back in the morning. Because it was almost one-thirty, only a handful of people were in the restaurant.

Josh was seated in a booth, reading the menu, when she slid breathlessly into the bench across from him. She really didn't have time to linger over lunch. She had a hundred things to do before the carnival opened at five.

"Sorry, I'm late," she said, glancing around for Miguel so they could order.

Josh reached for her hand. He'd changed out of his business suit and was dressed in slacks and a shirt, with the top two buttons left undone. He looked no less attractive in casual clothes—and maybe more so.

"You didn't have any problem finding your way around, did you?" she asked, using a chip to scoop up some salsa. Miguel seemed to be busy in the kitchen.

"You're joking, aren't you?" He laughed as he said it. "There's only one road through town."

There were more, but apparently he hadn't felt any

need to investigate the side streets.

"The other end of town is blocked off for the carnival," she reminded him. The motel and restaurant were located at this end of Red Springs.

"Have you decided what you'd like to eat?" she asked.

"I have."

As if he suddenly realized Joy had arrived, Miguel appeared to take their order. "I'll have the luncheon special. I can have the chili relleno baked, right?" Josh asked.

"We cook them the regular way," Miguel said in a heavy accent.

"Baked or fried?" Josh pressed.

Miguel looked to Joy to supply the answer.

"I believe they fry them, Josh," she said.

Josh frowned. "In that case, I'll have the enchilada plate."

Miguel gratefully wrote that down and turned to Joy, who nodded. He went back to the kitchen.

"Aren't you going to order?" Josh asked.

"I already did. I always have the same thing and Miguel knows how I like my tostada salad."

Josh reached out to clasp both her hands. "You look fabulous," he said, studying her. "Really fabulous."

She smiled at his words.

"I thought you'd come running home three months after you accepted this job," Josh admitted.

That wasn't exactly a flattering comment, but she let it slide.

"It's hard to believe you actually live here, so far from civilization," Josh added, glancing around as if he couldn't quite picture her in this setting.

"I remember thinking that when I first got to Red Springs. But it grew on me. I love it now."

"Don't you miss all the great restaurants in Seattle?"

"Well, yes, but . . ."

"This place is hardly Mexican," Josh murmured under his breath.

"The Mexican Fiesta isn't as fancy as the big chains in Seattle, but I like their food," she said, struggling not to sound defensive. She remembered her first visit to Red Springs. She'd wanted to live in a small community, but it had taken a while to adjust to the lack of amenities. The first time she'd eaten the town's version of Mexican food, she'd had to make an effort not to compare it to her favorite Seattle restaurant.

"We used to have Mexican food almost every week," Josh said.

Joy didn't think it had been that often.

He wrinkled his forehead. "If I recall correctly, you used to order chicken enchiladas."

That was definitely some other girl he'd dated. Joy had never really liked enchiladas. He'd probably seen a dozen different women in the last two years, culminating in his now-ended relationship with Lori.

"You'd better tell me how everything's going to work this afternoon," he said. "I hear this town's going to be rocking."

Joy detected a hint of condescension but ignored it.

She simply nodded. "Everyone within a fifty-mile radius shows up. Ranching's a hard way to make a living these days," she said, remembering her many conversations with Letty. "There are only a few occasions during the year when the community has cause for celebration, and the end of school is one."

"My mother never celebrated my getting out of school for the summer," he joked. "If anything, she was crying in her martini. No more tennis dates for her when Julie and I were underfoot all day."

"A lot of these kids help around the ranch," she explained. "Families are important here. Tradition, too."

Josh's parents had split up and both had remarried by the time he started junior high. Fractured households seemed natural to him, and a community like this, with its emphasis on strong families, would seem an anomaly in his world.

"Everyone's thrilled about the carnival rides," Joy said. "This is the first year we're doing that." The children's excitement at such a modest pleasure wasn't something Josh would understand or appreciate, so Joy didn't bother to explain it further.

For the next few minutes until their lunches arrived, they chatted about Red Springs and her role in the community. Miguel delivered their orders with his usual fanfare, and Joy sensed that Josh was restraining a sarcastic smile. Her tostada salad was exactly the way she liked it, but she noticed that he just stared at his enchiladas.

"A high school dance," he repeated when she reminded him that he'd agreed to chaperone with her. Clearly he was amused.

"Come on, it'll be fun."

"I'm sure it will." His eyes twinkled as he took the first bite of his enchiladas.

"Tell me about your job," she said, wanting to turn the subject away from herself.

Josh had always been easy to talk to, and she was soon immersed in their conversation. He liked working for the investment firm, where he seemed to be advancing quickly. He'd purchased a home in Kirkland, outside Seattle. This she knew from the e-mails they'd exchanged. He described in some detail what it meant to be a home owner.

As he spoke, Joy realized that, despite her earlier decision, she couldn't imagine living in Seattle again. Josh was proud of his home and she was happy for him, yet she knew that living in Red Springs had changed her. His kind of neighborhood, with its expensive homes and anonymity, was no longer what she wanted. Neither was his social life—company functions and cocktail parties at which barbed remarks passed for wit.

"What if you have to move?" she asked. His company was well-known; with his ambition and energy Josh might be asked to relocate to a different city.

"I like living in Seattle. However, if the firm asked me to change offices, and it came with a big promotion, I'd definitely consider it," he said.

Joy nodded.

"What about you?"

"Me? You mean, would I move if the opportunity arose?"

He seemed intensely interested in her answer. With his elbows propped on the table and his fork dangling over his food, he awaited her response.

"From Red Springs?" She swallowed. "I don't know. . . . I've settled in nicely and I feel like I'm part of the community." She'd be viewed as a newcomer for the next sixty years, but that didn't bother her.

"If a once-in-a-lifetime opportunity came up, how would you feel?"

"That would depend on the opportunity," she said, sidestepping the question.

The restaurant door opened and sunlight shot into the darkened room. Joy didn't pay much attention until Lonny strolled directly to her table.

"Hello, Joy," he said.

She nearly dropped her fork. Fortunately, she hadn't taken a sip of her water or she could've been in serious danger of choking.

"Lonny." His name was more breath than sound.

"Would you introduce me to your friend?" he asked, staring down at Josh.

"Uh . . ."

Josh slid out of the booth and stood. "Josh Howell," he said, extending his hand. "And you are?"

Lonny grinned as the two men exchanged handshakes. "Lonny Ellison. I'm the man who's in love with Joy."

Chapter Nineteen

Lonny nearly burst out laughing at the look on Joy's face.

"And how does Joy feel about you?" Josh asked coolly, before she managed to speak.

"She loves me, too, only she's not ready to admit it."

"Lonny!" Her fork fell to the table with a loud clang.

Lonny sent a glance at Josh and winked. "See what I mean?" The other man seemed to be somewhat taken aback but not angry, which boded well.

"What are you *doing* here?" Joy asked when it became apparent that he had no intention of leaving.

"Actually, Betty Sanders sent me to look for you," he told her. "She needs you for something, and Myrtle Jameson said she saw you come in here. There's a carnival that has to be set up, you know."

"I can see word spreads quickly in this town," Josh said, "if people are keeping track of your whereabouts."

Joy grabbed her purse and scrambled out of the booth. "I'll be right back."

As soon as she vacated the seat, Lonny replaced her. He was a bit hungry himself and selected a tortilla chip, dipping it in the salsa. "Take your time," he said nonchalantly. "I'll keep your friend company."

"I . . . I—" She was sputtering again. "I'll be back in five minutes," she promised Josh, and then returned to the table and kissed his cheek.

That, Lonny thought, was completely unnecessary; it

was more as if she had a point to prove. He looked away before she could see how deeply that small display of affection for another man had affected him.

"Nice to meet you, Josh," Lonny said when Joy was gone, "but I can't stay long. My sister's got me helping, too. My hired hand and I are assembling the beanbag toss. You'd think two grown men could put this silly contraption together, wouldn't you? The problem is, the instructions are in Chinese." He left the booth and started to walk out of the restaurant.

"Do you need help with that?" Josh called after him.

"Thanks, but I think we've got it. A couple of others could use a hand, though."

Josh nodded. "I'll settle up here and be out soon."

"Thanks," Lonny said. Despite the fact that Josh was here to reconnect with the woman *he* loved, Lonny decided he rather liked him. He seemed to be a decent guy.

When he stepped outside, Lonny saw Joy trotting down the sidewalk, toward the restaurant. She ignored him and kept moving.

"Did you find her?" Tom asked, when Lonny got back to the carnival site. The beanbag toss apparatus was up but balanced precariously, leaning to one side. They had to find a way to stabilize it.

"Cricket and I finished with the Go Fish booth," Chase announced triumphantly, carrying the little girl on his shoulders and joining Lonny and Tom.

Cricket smiled down at them from her perch. "We did a good job, too."

"Cricket," Letty cried, rushing toward them, hands on her hips. "Chase, put her down right this minute."

Lonny was grateful to see his sister. "I saw Joy," he said, striving to sound unconcerned.

Letty lifted her brows in question.

"She was with Josh Howell," Lonny added.

"He *said* he was her boyfriend," Cricket muttered indignantly. "He isn't, is he?" The question was directed at her uncle.

"No way," Lonny assured the little girl.

"Then how come he said that?"

The kid had a point. "He just doesn't know it yet," Lonny explained, not meeting Letty's eyes.

"Miss Fuller will tell him, won't she?"

"She will soon enough," Lonny said.

"However," Letty cut in, "Miss Fuller is the one making the decisions, not your Uncle Lonny."

Cricket waited for Lonny to agree or disagree. Lonny shrugged. His sister wasn't wrong, but the situation was more complicated than that.

Letty was frowning. "Listen, we don't have time to stand here discussing Joy's love life. The carnival's about to start."

"All right, all right." Lonny picked up the beanbag toss instructions once again. He studied the drawing, turned it around and took another look. Ah, that made more sense.

By five o'clock, the streets of Red Springs were filled to capacity. This was probably the one time of year when the town got a taste of big-city living, complete with traffic jams. Parking slots were at a premium. Many streets were closed off and teeming with kids and adults alike, all enjoying themselves.

Chase and Lonny took a shift together, grilling hamburgers and serving them as quickly as they were cooked. While he was flipping burgers, Lonny caught a glimpse of Joy out of the corner of his eye. She was strolling through the grounds with Josh, sharing a bag of popcorn and sipping lemonade. He pretended not to notice but his gut tightened, and almost immediately the doubts began chasing each other, around and around. Maybe Josh would convince her, after all. Just as fast, a sense of well-being returned. Joy had as much pride as he did, but she wasn't stupid. She loved him. Lonny believed that . . . and yet there were a lot of factors he hadn't considered before. Such as the fact that Josh was so likeable and that Joy had family and friends in Seattle. Josh could offer her a more privileged life. All the reasons marriage to Josh made sense presented themselves to his fevered mind.

Lonny's gut remained in knots until he saw Tom and Michelle stroll past, holding hands. His mood instantly lightened. This carnival was probably Tom's first real date. Tom kept his emotions in check about most things, but he hadn't been able to squelch his enthusiasm for the carnival and the high school dance that was to follow. The kid had his chores finished before the sun was even up. He was ready to leave for town by ten that morning. Lonny had to assign him some extra work to keep him busy and distracted from his anxieties about Michelle. By two o'clock, though, he was dressed and waiting.

Apparently Michelle had informed him it wasn't necessary to wear a suit to the dance, so Tom had given it back to Lonny. The kid's eyes had lit up like Christmas morning when Lonny assured him he didn't need it anymore. He told Tom to keep the suit because he might be able to use it someday. Tom had purchased a new shirt and jeans for the dance and he'd even had his hair cut and he'd polished his black boots to a shine they'd likely never seen before.

Michelle had been good for Tom. She'd talked to him about college, reinforcing Lonny's suggestions, and encouraged him to apply for scholarships. Together Tom and Lonny had worked on completing the on-line application forms. Lonny felt pleased that Tom was looking beyond his past and toward the future.

In the same way Michelle had helped Tom, Joy had been good for Lonny. While it was true that they'd argued frequently, Joy had taught Lonny some important things about himself. Not the least of which was the knowledge that he wanted marriage and family. That was a new aspiration for him.

The moment he and Chase finished their shift, he planned to seek her out. He couldn't stand by and do nothing while Josh escorted her about town. That went against every dictate of his will.

Caught up in his own anxiety, he automatically followed Chase to the long line of kids waiting for cotton candy. Only after a few minutes did he realize his sister was the one stirring up the sugary pink confection.

When Letty saw Lonny, she motioned for him to come to the front of the line.

"Don't do it," she said, looking at him sternly. Her mouth was pinched and she resembled their mother more than he'd thought possible.

"Do what?" he asked, playing innocent.

"Don't play games with me, big brother. I know you." All the while she was speaking, Letty rotated the paper cone along the outside of the circular barrel as it produced the cotton candy. *"Stay way from Joy."* Smiling, she took two tickets from the waiting youngster and handed her the fluffy pink bouquet.

"But—"

"Chase, don't you *dare* let him go near Joy while she's with Josh."

Chase frowned. "I'm not his baby-sitter."

"Stay with him. You can do that, can't you?"

Chase obviously wasn't happy about it. "I suppose."

"Good."

"Here," she said, giving Lonny a tube of cotton candy. "Both of you stay out of trouble, okay?"

Feeling like a kid who'd just been reprimanded, Lonny nodded. "I took your advice earlier. I suppose I can again." He just hoped Letty recognized how difficult this was going to be.

His sister narrowed her eyes. "Listen to me, Lonny," she insisted. "You've got to let Joy make up her own mind."

"But . . ."

"If you push her, you'll lose her. Understand?"

Lonny sighed. What choice did he have?

Chase took Cricket to all the kids' rides and Lonny felt like a third wheel walking around with the two of them. Every now and then, he unexpectedly caught a glimpse of Joy and Josh. Once he saw them deep in conversation, their heads close together as they shared the bag of popcorn. Josh fed Joy a kernel and she smiled up at him as she accepted it.

Lonny's stomach convulsed at the sight. It came to him then that Josh might actually have the upper hand. He'd been so certain earlier, convinced to the core that Joy Fuller loved *him*. Now he wasn't nearly as sure.

Confronted with Joy and Josh looking so comfortable, so intimate, was a rude awakening. Letty seemed to think doing nothing was the best response. It was killing him, but so far he'd managed. Barely.

"You okay?" Chase asked at one point.

"No," Lonny admitted from between clenched teeth. It began to seem that every time he turned a corner, there was Joy with her college boyfriend. When he saw them holding hands, he involuntarily started toward her. Chase grabbed his elbow, stopping him.

"Remember what Letty said," his friend muttered.

"How would *you* feel?" Lonny snapped, glaring at him.

"If I saw Letty holding hands with another man, you mean?" Chase asked. He shook his head. "Same way you're feeling now."

"That's what I thought."

"Josh will be on his way back to Seattle in a day, maybe two, and that'll be the end of it."

With all his heart, Lonny wanted to believe that Joy would stay. "But what if she decides to go with him?" he asked. The possibility seemed very real at the moment.

"If she does, then it was meant to be."

Chase sounded so casual about it. So offhand. Apparently the love Lonny had for Joy didn't figure into this. Not according to his friend, anyway. Lonny didn't know how he was supposed to just keep his mouth shut and pretend Chase was right. Like hell she'd leave with Josh What's-his-name! He'd fight for Joy, make her understand how deep his feelings ran. He wasn't a man who gave his heart easily. He wasn't going to stand idly by and watch Josh walk off with her. Not in this lifetime. Not ever.

"You can't force her to marry you," Chase said, his hold tightening on Lonny's elbow.

"Sure I can," Lonny argued, for argument's sake.

Chase's response was to laugh.

"All right, all right," Lonny reluctantly agreed. He had to let this play out the way it would. The decision was up to her, and Lonny tried to believe that her good sense—and her true feelings—would prevail.

"The dance starts in an hour," Chase reminded him.

"Thank God for that." At least there he wouldn't be exposed to the sight of Joy and Josh holding hands and whispering to each other. He'd be able to concentrate on the kids and forget that his life was on the verge of imploding.

The dance was held in the high school gymnasium. Lonny got there early to avoid the risk of seeing Joy with Josh again. There was a limit to how much torture he could take.

The high school kids had done an admirable job of decorating the basketball court. The student body obviously had enough funds to hire a real band. Well, a live band, anyway. They were tuning up, and discordant sounds spilled out the open doors. Grimacing, Lonny had to resist plugging his ears. He just hoped Tom appreciated his sacrifice. Actually, he should be the one thanking Tom for an excuse to leave that blasted carnival. No telling how long those festivities would last.

Couples were slowly drifting in. While the guys were dressed in jeans and Western shirts, the girls all seemed to be wearing fancy dresses and strappy high-heeled shoes. If there'd been a dance like this while he was in school, Lonny didn't remember it. Sitting at the back of the gymnasium, guarding the punch bowl, he saw Tom and Michelle arrive.

Charley Larson's daughter was lovely. She wore a corsage on her wrist, and Lonny knew Tom had worried plenty about that white rose. But all his anguish and fretting seemed worth it now. They exuded such innocent happiness, Lonny found himself smiling.

Then, just when he'd started to relax, he saw Joy. He froze with a cup of punch halfway to his mouth. Sure enough, Josh tagged along behind her, his hand on her waist. Lonny felt as if someone had stuck a knife in his back. This dance was supposed to be his escape. Instead, it was fast becoming the scene of his emotional downfall. He didn't know how he'd manage to stand by and do nothing when Josh took Joy in his arms. Joy, the woman Lonny loved and hoped to marry.

The music began in earnest then. The lead singer stepped up to the microphone and announced the first dance.

Lonny set aside his punch and marched across the room.

When Joy saw him she scowled fiercely. "What are *you* doing here?" she demanded. She seemed to be asking that a lot today.

"I'm a chaperone. And you?"

"We're chaperoning, as well," Josh answered on her behalf.

Couples surged onto the dance floor all around them. "I believe this dance is mine," Lonny said and held out his hand to Joy.

She met his gaze without flinching, but didn't respond. She glanced at Josh, as if to ask his permission.

"Would you mind if I danced this one number with Joy?" Lonny kept his voice as free of emotion as possible.

"Go ahead."

Lonny half expected Joy to argue with him and was

pleasantly surprised when she simply followed him onto the dance floor. Since this was the first such event Lonny had chaperoned, he didn't know if the adults were allowed to dance. That, however, didn't concern him. If they wanted to fire him, they could. He didn't care. All that mattered was having Joy in his arms again.

He took her hand and she moved reluctantly into his arms. To his relief, this was a slow dance. Closing his eyes, Lonny brought her against him and noticed how stiff she was.

"I don't know what you think you're doing," she whispered heatedly.

He pretended not to hear. Despite her reluctance, he drew her closer and held her hand in his.

"I'm talking to you," she said. "Could you answer me?"

Lonny ignored her question. A minute or two later, he felt her relax slightly. After that, it didn't take long for her to sigh and begin to move with him.

This was what he wanted, what he *needed*. Her body flowed naturally in motion with his. The fear started to leave him and he tightened his arm around her waist. This was perfect. They even breathed in unison.

Although it was torture of a different kind not to kiss her, when the music stopped, Lonny dropped his arms and stepped back.

"Thank you."

Joy stared at him, her eyes wide and confused.

He held her gaze for a long moment, unable to look

away. It was on the tip of his tongue to remind her how much he loved her.

But Joy abruptly turned then and walked back to Josh, who stood waiting on the sidelines.

Chapter Twenty

Joy wanted to argue with Lonny. He'd purposely gone out of his way to embarrass her, first in the restaurant and now on the dance floor. Understandably, Josh had asked plenty of questions this afternoon. Joy had explained her complicated relationship with Lonny as well as she could. He'd listened, but hadn't pressured her. He'd responded as a friend would, and for that she was grateful. Joy had seen Lonny watching them at the carnival. Every time she looked up, he seemed to be there, his gaze following her like a hawk tracking its prey.

Then, to confuse the situation even more, Lonny had to insist on dancing with her. That was when the *real* trouble started. She'd expected him to argue with her, which would've been fine. Joy was more than ready to give him an earful. All afternoon she'd felt his disapproving gaze. And then, when they'd danced . . .

Joy had expected him to coerce her and exploit his advantage. But even while her mind whirled with an angry torrent of accusations, her body seemed to melt in his arms. Somehow, without her being aware of it, her eyes had closed and her head was pressed against his shoulder. He hadn't uttered a single word. All Lonny had done was hold her, dance with her. When the music stopped, he'd simply released her.

She moved slowly to the edge of the floor.

"I believe the next dance is mine," Josh said as he came forward to claim Joy.

"Yes, of—of course," she stammered. Absorbed in her thoughts, she hadn't noticed that Josh had approached her. The music began again.

"That would be . . ." She couldn't think of the right word. *Nice,* she mused, as Josh took her hand and led her onto the floor. The music was much faster this time, and the dance floor quickly became crowded.

Josh was an accomplished dancer. His movements were flamboyant, energetic but controlled—as good as anything she'd ever seen in music videos. The teenagers gathered around him were clapping in time with the music. More and more people came to watch his performance, and it occurred to Joy that he wasn't dancing with *her,* the way Lonny had. They were just occupying the same space. She tried gamely to keep up with him. Joy was impressed with his dancing, all the while disliking that the two of them were the center of attention.

Joy had gone to a number of dances with Josh during their college days, but she couldn't remember his being this smooth or agile. Apparently, it was a recently acquired skill.

The music stopped, and the crowd broke into spontaneous applause. Joy couldn't get off the floor fast enough. Josh followed her, but at a slower pace.

"Where did you learn to dance like that?" Joy asked, and realized there was a lot about him she no longer knew. Josh had changed; the thing was, Joy had, too.

"Lori and I danced a lot."

"You're great at it," Joy said sincerely. This was the first real dance she'd attended in two years and frankly, she could do with a refresher course. Beside Josh, she'd looked pretty lame, she thought ruefully. But there just weren't that many opportunities to dance in Red Springs. Most places served beer in jugs, played only country-western music and had floors covered with sawdust.

Josh's smile didn't quite reach his eyes. "I miss it, you know."

Joy suspected it was more than the dancing Josh missed, but she kept her opinions to herself.

When she looked up, she saw that Lonny was watching her again.

Because she had a job to do, she walked along the perimeter of the dance floor, her eyes focused on the dancing couples. Josh strolled beside her. She noticed Tom, Lonny's hired hand, and Michelle Larson dancing together. Tom appeared awkward and uneasy, concentrating heavily on each movement. He was rigid and held Michelle an arm's length away from him. His lips moved as he silently counted the steps. Michelle, bless her, tried her best to follow his lead. They were a sweet-looking couple.

A moment later, Joy saw that she wasn't the only one

watching Tom and Michelle dance. Kenny Brighton stood at the outer edge of the dance floor, eyeing the couple, his fists flexing at his sides.

Joy felt it was her duty to waylay trouble before it happened. Trying not to be obvious, she moved toward the other boy, pulling Josh with her, holding his hand.

"Good evening, Kenny," she said. "May I introduce you to my friend, Josh Howell?"

Kenny didn't appreciate the interruption in his brooding. He acknowledged her with the faintest of nods, but his gaze didn't waver from Tom and Michelle.

"Kenny's family helped bring the carnival rides to Red Springs," Joy said brightly to Josh, as though this was a feat worthy of mention. "Isn't that right, Kenny?" she added when he didn't respond.

"If you say so," he muttered.

"Is there a problem between you and Tom?" she asked, deciding it was best to confront the issue head-on. Subtlety was getting them nowhere.

For the first time Kenny tore his eyes away from the dancing couple. "Michelle was supposed to be *my* date."

"You mean to say Tom kidnapped her?" she asked, making light of the situation. Her laugh fell decidedly flat.

Kenny wasn't amused. "Something like that. I asked her first and she had some weak excuse for why she couldn't go with me. Next thing I hear, she's coming to the dance with Ellison's ranch hand." He practically spat the last two words.

"That's a woman's prerogative, isn't it?" Joy said, desperately hoping to keep the peace. This was the last official school event of the year, and she didn't want to see it ruined.

Kenny didn't appear to agree with her. "I'm twice the man that hired hand will ever be."

"Kenny, listen, we don't want any trouble here," she said, turning to Josh for help.

Josh nodded. "Why don't you find someone else to dance with," he suggested.

Kenny turned to Josh long enough to cast him a look of disdain. "I don't want to," he said sullenly. Joy could smell alcohol on his breath, strictly forbidden but furtively indulged in by the older boys.

She was afraid of what Kenny might do next, afraid he'd welcome an opportunity to fight Tom again. In his current frame of mind, Kenny might even see Josh as a convenient target, ridiculous though that was.

"Come on," Josh said, urging her away from Kenny. "I don't think you can do any good here."

Joy was reluctant to leave. As she moved past Kenny, she noticed Lonny keeping a close eye on the boy, too. He darted a look in her direction and she nodded, glancing at Kenny. Lonny's faint smile assured her he had matters well in hand.

Joy was astonished at how effectively they were able to communicate with just eye contact. This was a difficult situation with the potential to blow up into a major fracas. At the same time, she had every confidence that Lonny would know how to handle it. Sighing with relief, she patrolled the dance floor, smiling at students she recognized. She exchanged greetings with the other chaperones, and when she introduced Josh, she noted several surprised looks. Lonny wasn't the only one who seemed to think she was linked to him romantically.

"Would you like to dance again?" Josh asked when they'd made their way completely around the dance floor. They stood near the punch bowl, while Lonny was on the other side of the room closest to Kenny. She kept her eyes trained on the boy in case a problem erupted. Not that there was much she'd be able to do . . .

"Joy?" Josh prodded.

"I'm not sure I should," she said.

Although she'd been out on the floor twice, making a spectacle of herself at least once, she was present at this event in an official capacity. She could sense trouble simmering and felt obliged to take her chaperoning duties more seriously. Still, she felt bad about abandoning Josh.

"I need to be aware of what's happening and I can't do that if I'm dancing," she mumbled, standing on her tiptoes and stretching to look for Kenny. He was gone.

"Don't worry," Josh said. "I understand."

She thanked him with a smile. "Feel free to ask one of the other chaperones to dance." Josh really had been a good sport about all of this. "Do you see Kenny any-place?"

Josh scanned the crowd. "No, I can't say I do."

Joy glanced around, looking for Tom and Michelle.

Her suspicions were instantly aroused. Without explaining, she dashed across the now-empty dance floor toward Lonny.

Lonny must have known immediately that something was wrong, because he met her halfway and reached for her hands.

"Kenny's missing," she gasped out, "and so is Tom."

Lonny released a harsh breath. "I saw Kenny leave but I thought Tom was with Michelle."

"He isn't. I just saw Michelle come out of the restroom."

Lonny didn't wait for her to say any more. He hurried off the dance floor and out of the building. Not knowing what else to do, Joy followed. She left Josh talking to a couple of other teachers—both women.

The first thing she saw when she got outside was that a group of kids, mostly boys, had clustered in a ragged circle. Joy couldn't see much of what was taking place but she heard an ugly din, interspersed by girls' screams. She nudged her way through the crowd, behind Lonny.

As soon as he broke through the crowd gathered to watch, Lonny burst into the middle.

Joy saw that two boys were holding Tom down while Kenny Brighton took a swing at him. Tom kicked and bucked against the youths restraining him. Michelle stood to one side with her hands covering her face, moaning, unable to watch.

"If there's going to be a fight, it'll be a fair one," Lonny roared.

Outrage filled Joy. From the murmurs she heard around her, she wasn't the only person who objected to what was going on. She was about to interrupt Lonny and insist that the fight be stopped altogether. But before she could say anything, Lonny rushed forward and tore the other boys off Tom. He flung them aside as if they were no more than flies.

Tom stood up, smudged with dirt and clutching his stomach. One eye was black, and the corner of his mouth was bleeding. Michelle ran forward, letting out a distressed cry as she saw Tom. Joy went over to the girl and placed one arm around her shoulders.

"What's your problem?" Lonny demanded, addressing Kenny.

"He stole my girlfriend," the larger boy shouted, his face twisted with rage. He raised his fists again as if eager to return to the pounding he'd been giving Tom.

"I'm not his girlfriend," Michelle shouted back.

"You were until he showed up," Kenny challenged, motioning toward Tom.

"You want to fight Tom?" Lonny asked.

Kenny nodded. "Let me at him, and I'll show you how much I want to fight."

"Tom?" Lonny asked.

Tom wiped the blood from his mouth with the back of his hand and nodded, too.

"Fine. Then step back, everyone, and give them plenty of room."

Joy couldn't believe what she was hearing. Lonny was actually condoning the fight! "No," she cried. Not only was she against physical violence, which in her view was never an appropriate response, but she could tell that even one on one, this wouldn't be a "fair" fight. She felt she needed to point out the obvious discrepancies in their sizes. "Lonny, no! Kenny outweighs Tom by thirty or forty pounds."

Lonny ignored her protest.

"Stay back, gentlemen," Lonny told the two boys who'd been holding Tom down.

It seemed the entire gymnasium had emptied onto the field by this point. Joy remained at Michelle's side, still horrified that Lonny was allowing the two boys to continue fighting.

"I've got to break this up!" she said urgently.

"No," Michelle said, stopping her. "I hate it, but this is the way things are settled here. Tom doesn't have any choice except to fight Kenny."

"He could get hurt." Joy knew Michelle didn't want to see Tom hurt any more than she did.

"Mr. Ellison won't let that happen," Michelle told her.

Although she'd been part of the community for two years, Joy didn't fully understand why some quarrels like this had to be handled by such primitive means. Besides, Lonny seemed to be setting Tom up for defeat. Kenny was bigger and stronger, and poor Tom didn't stand a chance.

Kenny came out swinging, eager to take Tom down with one swift blow. To Joy's surprise, Tom nimbly ducked, and Kenny's powerful swing met nothing but air. The larger boy stumbled forward, and that was when Tom thrust his fist up and struck, hitting Kenny squarely in the jaw.

Kenny whirled back, a look of shock on his face.

"You ready to call it quits?" Tom asked him.

"Not on your life, you little weasel." Kenny swung again, with the same result.

This time, Tom drove a fist into Kenny's stomach, and the other boy doubled over.

"I'm not as easy to hit without someone holding me down, am I?" Tom said scornfully.

Joy loosened her grip on Michelle's shoulders, suspecting the fight was almost over. The girl took a deep shuddering breath.

Twice more Kenny Brighton went after Tom. Both times Tom was too quick for him. Whenever Kenny took a swing, Tom retaliated with a solid punch, until Kenny lowered his arms and shook his head.

"You finished?" Lonny asked, stepping forward.

Kenny nodded.

"Is this the end of it?" Lonny stood between them.

Tom nodded and Kenny did, too, reluctantly.

"Then shake hands."

Tom came forward with his hand extended and Kenny met him halfway.

"I don't have to like you," Kenny bit out.

"Same here," Tom said.

They stared at each other, then wearily backed away.

Michelle immediately rushed to Tom's side and slipped her arm around his waist. "Are you all right?"

"I'm fine," he said smiling. "Are we going to dance or not?"

"Dance," she replied, and her eyes sparkled with delight. "Oh, Tom, I would never have guessed you could hold your own against Kenny."

They returned to the gym and in a few minutes, the crowd dwindled. Kenny's friends gathered around him, but he brusquely pushed them aside and stalked to the parking lot.

"Is it over?" Joy asked Lonny, still a little nervous.

"There's nothing to worry about now," he assured her.

"I don't understand why they had to fight." Nothing like this would've been allowed anywhere else; she was convinced of that. Certainly not at a school in Seattle.

"You didn't see any of the other chaperones stopping the fight, did you?"

Joy had to agree she hadn't.

"This way it was fair and there were witnesses. Kenny learned a valuable lesson tonight, and my guess is it's one he won't soon forget."

Joy wasn't nearly as convinced of that as Lonny seemed to be.

"He'll go home and lick his wounds," Lonny continued. "Basically, Kenny's a good kid. It embarrassed him to lose, especially in front of his friends—and the girl he likes."

"What was the lesson he supposedly learned?" Joy

asked, not quite restraining her sarcasm.

Lonny looked at her in puzzlement. "Kenny learned that being bigger and stronger isn't necessarily an advantage," he said as though that should be obvious.

"Yes, but—"

"He was humiliated in front of his classmates because they saw that it took two of his friends to hold Tom down in order for Kenny to get in a hit. No one wants to be known as a dirty fighter."

"But . . ."

"He won't make the same mistake twice. Kenny might not like Tom, but now, at least, he respects him."

Joy just shook her head. "I don't understand fighting and I never will."

"You're new here," he said with a shrug, as if that explained everything.

"In other words, I don't belong in Red Springs."

Lonny smiled. "I wouldn't say that, but I would definitely say you belong with me."

Joy walked slowly back to the dance, where she found Josh in the middle of the floor, once again the center of attention.

Chapter Twenty-One

As part of the carnival cleanup committee, Lonny got to town early the next morning. Tom accompanied him, but Lonny was under no delusion—the attraction wasn't sweeping the streets. Tom had come with the express purpose of finding Michelle Larson. Lonny was just as eager for a glimpse of Joy.

It was clear to him that Joy and Josh were completely incompatible, and he hoped she finally had the good sense to recognize it. After two years in Red Springs, Joy had become a country girl. Life in the big city was no longer right for her. According to what Letty had told him, Josh would be leaving Red Springs in a day or two. Soon, in other words, but not soon enough to suit Lonny.

Broom in hand, he walked down Main Street, sweeping up trash as he went. The carnival people had already packed their equipment, ready to move on to the next town.

Red Springs was taking its time waking up after a late night. Uncle Dave's, the local café, didn't hang out the "open" sign until after seven-thirty. Their biscuits and gravy, with a cup of strong coffee, was the best breakfast in town. Whenever he had the chance, Lonny sat at the counter and ordered a double portion of the house special. Those biscuits would carry him all the way to evening.

He was busy dumping trash into a large plastic bag when he noticed Josh Howell leaving the restaurant, holding a cup of takeout coffee.

"How's it going?" Josh said, approaching Lonny. He surveyed the street, where the majority of the festivities had taken place.

"All right, I guess." Lonny stopped sweeping and leaned against the broom. He liked the other man, but if it came to stepping aside so Josh could walk off with Joy, well, that was another matter.

"You said you love Joy," Josh murmured.

"I do."

Josh nodded soberly. "She's in love with you, too." He looked down at his feet and then up again. "The entire time we were together, she was watching you. She couldn't take her eyes off you."

It demanded severe discipline on Lonny's part not to leap into the air and click his cowboy boots in jubilation.

"I'm not sure Joy realizes it yet," Josh added.

Lonny disagreed. "She knows it, all right—only she isn't happy about it."

Josh grinned as if he agreed. "I'll be heading back to Seattle later this morning. Earlier than I intended, but I can see the lay of the land. It's obvious that Joy and I don't have a future together." He met Lonny's eyes. "Good luck."

Lonny extended his arm and the two exchanged handshakes.

"Are you planning to marry her?" Josh surprised him by asking next.

Lonny had thought of little else all week. "I am, just as soon as she'll have me." He didn't know how long it would take Joy to listen to reason. But with a decision this important, he could be a patient man—even if patience didn't come naturally.

Josh left soon afterward and Lonny, Tom and the others spent the better part of two hours finishing their task. He was near-starved by that time, so he stopped off at Uncle Dave's for a huge plate of biscuits and gravy. Tom joined him.

When they'd cleaned their plates, Tom made an excuse to visit the feed store. That was fine with Lonny. He had personal business to attend to himself, and he was eager to do it. He just hoped Josh had already left town.

But when Lonny pulled up in front of Joy's place, he discovered, to his disappointment, that her PT Cruiser wasn't parked out front. That wasn't a good sign.

He hadn't expected to feel nervous, but he did. He'd had plenty of romances before Joy; however, this was the first time he'd planned on asking a woman to share his life. To show the seriousness of his intentions, he should probably present her with a ring—except that he didn't have one. His mother's diamond was in the safety deposit box at the bank. Although it had minimal financial worth, its sentimental value was incalculable.

Pulling away from the curb, Lonny glanced at his watch and saw that he only had a few minutes to catch Walt Abler before the bank closed at noon, which it did on Saturdays. In his rush, Lonny forgot about the stop sign at Spruce and Oak and shot past it. A flash of red caught his attention just before a little green PT Cruiser barreled into his line of vision. Lonny slammed on his brakes, but it was too late. He would have broadsided the Cruiser if not for the quick thinking of the other driver, who steered left to avoid a collision. Unfortunately, the green car's bumper scraped against the stop sign post.

Lonny's heart was in his throat, and he held the steering wheel in a death grip, reflecting on what a narrow escape he'd had.

"What the hell do you think you're doing?" Joy Fuller shrieked as she climbed out of her vehicle and banged the door shut with enough strength to jam it for good.

Lonny had guessed it was Joy the minute he saw the green car. He got out of the driver's seat and rushed over to her side.

"Are you okay?" he demanded.

"Yes, no thanks to you."

"I'm sorry. I don't know what I was thinking. I forgot the stop sign was there." His excuse was weak, but it was the truth.

Apparently Joy hadn't even heard him. "Look what you've done to my car!" She sounded close to tears as she examined the damage to her bumper.

The dent was barely noticeable as far as Lonny could see. He walked over and ran his hand along her bumper frame and then stepped back.

"This is a new car," she cried.

"I thought you got it last year."

"I did. But it's still new to me and now you've, you've—"

"Have it fixed. I'll pay for it."

"You're darn right you will." She raised her hand to her forehead.

Fearing she might have hit her head, Lonny took her

by the shoulders and turned her to face him. "Are you okay?" he asked again.

She nodded.

"You didn't hit your head?"

"I . . . I don't think so."

"Maybe you should sit down for a minute to be sure." The fact that she was willing to comply was worry enough. Sitting on the curb, Joy drew in several deep breaths. Lonny welcomed the opportunity to calm his own heart, which was beating at an accelerated pace.

"Where were you going in such an all-fired hurry?" she asked after a moment. She bolted suddenly to her feet.

"The bank. But what does it matter where I was going?" he asked, standing, too.

"You can't drive like that in town! You're an accident waiting to happen."

"I . . . I—" He didn't know what to say. The accident *had* been his fault. All at once he realized that just a few weeks earlier, their situations had been reversed. She'd caused the same kind of mishap and he'd been the one demanding answers to almost identical questions.

"You should have your driver's license suspended for being so irresponsible." Arms akimbo, she faced him, eyes flashing.

"Now, Joy . . ."

"I should contact the Department of Motor Vehicles myself."

"Joy." He was doing his level best to remain calm. "Getting upset like this isn't good."

"Don't tell me what I can and can't do!"

"Okay, fine, do whatever you want."

"I will," she snapped and started to stomp away.

He didn't want her to leave, not like this. "I love you, you know."

She paused, her back to him. Finally, she turned around, a thoughtful frown on her face. "You're sure about that?"

He nodded. "Very sure. Fact is, I was on my way to pick up an engagement ring."

Her frown darkened. "You said you were going to the bank."

"I was. My mother's diamond wedding ring is in the vault there. I intended to give you that. You can change the setting if you wish."

Joy seemed stunned into speechlessness.

"Letty wanted Mom's pearls and insisted I keep the ring in case I decided to get married. She was thinking my wife-to-be would like that diamond." He was rambling, but he couldn't seem to stop himself. "It's not a big stone. It's just a plain, ordinary diamond, but Mom loved it." He glanced at his watch again. "I'll have to wait until Monday now, and then you can see for yourself."

"A diamond ring?" From the look on her face, Lonny wondered if Joy had understood a single word he'd said.

"Now probably isn't the time or place to ask you to be my wife." Letty had been telling him all along that he had a terrible sense of timing.

"No . . . no, I disagree," Joy said. "Continue, please."

Since she seemed prepared to listen, Lonny figured he should take this opportunity. He cleared his throat and removed his hat. "Will you?"

She blinked and craned her neck toward him. "Will I *what?*"

"Marry me." He thought it was obvious.

"That's it?" She threw her arms in the air. *"Will you?"*

He didn't see the problem. "Yes."

"This is the most important question of a woman's life, Lonny Ellison."

"It's damned important to a man, too," he said.

"I want a little more than *will you.*"

Annoyed with her tone, he glared at her. "Do you want me to add *please?* Is that it?"

"That would be an improvement."

"All right. *Please.*"

She motioned as if asking him to come closer. "And?"

"You mean you want *more?*" Lonny had never expected a marriage proposal to be this difficult. He wished now that he'd talked to his brother-in-law first. Chase would've advised him on the proper protocol.

"Of course." Joy didn't sound too patient. "For starters, why do you want to marry me?"

That was a question he was beginning to ask himself. "I already told you—I love you."

"Okay. That's a good start."

"Start?" The woman exasperated him. "What else is there?"

"Quite a bit, as it happens."

Lonny shook his head. "Are you interested or not? Because this is getting downright ridiculous."

Joy folded her arms and cocked her head to one side, as if to consider the question. "I might be, if the person doing the asking put a little more of his heart into the proposal."

Exhaling, Lonny looked up at the sky and prayed for tolerance. "Joy Fuller, the luckiest day of my life was the day you ran me off the road, because that was when I discovered how much I love you."

She narrowed her eyes, apparently not sure she should believe him.

"I didn't know it then," he went on. "In fact, I didn't know it for a long time. This might be news, but I'm not in the habit of kissing unwilling females. You were the first."

"And the last," she inserted.

"The absolute last," he agreed. "I kissed you because you made me so crazy I didn't know how else to respond. I understand now that it wasn't anger I was feeling. It was attraction so strong it simply knocked me off my feet."

"Well, you infuriated *me*."

Lonny grinned at that. "This isn't the best way to go about reconciling," he said.

She conceded with a curt nod.

Lonny stepped closer and reached for her hands, holding them in his. "I don't know that much about love. I've been a bachelor so long, I'd sort of assumed

I'd always be one. Since meeting you, I've found I don't want to be alone anymore."

Her eyes went liquid with tenderness. "Really?"

"I don't need you to cook and clean and that other stuff. I don't care about that. I've been doing those things myself, anyway." He didn't like housework and Tom didn't, either, but between the two of them they managed.

"Then why do you want me?"

"I'd like you to sit on the porch with me in the evenings, the way my parents used to do. I like telling you my ideas and listening to what you think. I want us to be partners. If Chase and I do go ahead with our guest-ranch idea, you'd be a real help because you know kids."

"*Are* you going to pursue that?"

"I haven't talked to him yet," he admitted, "but whether we do or not, I still want you as my wife."

She nodded slowly.

"Speaking of kids," he said, "I'd like a few and I hope you would, too." He should probably clarify his feelings on the matter right now. "I've seen you with the children at school, and Cricket thinks the world of you. Letty, too. As far as I'm concerned, you couldn't have any better character witnesses. They love you and I'm just falling into line behind them."

Joy gave him a quavery smile. "I want children, too."

"I was thinking a couple of kids. Maybe three."

Lonny recalled the dream he'd had of two little boys and a girl, and just the memory of it tightened his gut with a mixture of love and longing. Intent on making this proposal as perfect as possible, Lonny raised her hand to his lips. "Joy Fuller, will you marry me?"

"Yes," she whispered and tears rolled down her cheeks.

"Soon?" he asked, then added, "Please."

She smiled at that and nodded.

His heart full, Lonny wrapped his arms around her and brought his mouth down on hers. He wanted this to be a gentle kiss, one that spoke of their love and commitment. Yet the moment her mouth met his, he thought he might explode. He wanted her with him, in his home and his bed, right then and there. Waiting even a day seemed too long.

Joy must have felt the same way, because she became fully involved in the kiss. She held nothing back, nothing at all.

By the time Lonny broke it off, they were both breathless. A car had stopped at the intersection—obeying the stop sign—and honked approvingly. Fortunately, traffic was unusually sparse for a Saturday.

"Wow," Lonny whispered, pressing his forehead against hers. "I could get a license first thing Monday morning, and we can be married by the end of the week."

"Lonny, Lonny, Lonny." Her eyes were warm with love as she straightened, shaking her head. "I only intend to get married once in my life, and I'm going to do it properly."

"Don't tell me you want a big wedding." He

should've known she was going to make a production of this.

"Yes, I want a wedding." She said this as if it should be a foregone conclusion. "Not necessarily *big,* but a real wedding."

This was already getting complicated. "Will I have to wear one of those fancy suits with a ruffled shirt?"

She laughed, but he wasn't joking. "That's negotiable."

"How long's the planning going to take?"

"A few weeks."

He groaned, hating the thought. "Weeks. You've got to be kidding."

Her look told him she wasn't. Then she smiled again, and it was one of the most beautiful smiles he'd ever seen. It was full of promise and love—and desire. When she kissed him, his knees went weak.

"I promise," she whispered, "that however long the planning takes, it'll be worth the wait."

With the next kiss, Lonny's doubts vanished.

Center Point Publishing
600 Brooks Road ● PO Box 1
Thorndike ME 04986-0001 USA

(207) 568-3717

US & Canada:
1 800 929-9108

DATE DUE